I0556208

Evan

A Novel by
CLIFTON LABREE

© 2015 by Author, Clifton LaBree

Published by
Fading Shadows Imprint
New Boston, New Hampshire, USA

Paperback ISBN-10: 1943329176
Paperback ISBN-13: 978-1-943329-17-5

Cover Design by Vivian LaBree

Dedicated to my wife Pauline, and my family, with thanks for all their support and encouragement.

Chapter One

Staff Sergeant Evan Mundy slowly read the letter one more time, viewing the words through a veil of tears:

Monson, Maine
November 10, 1918

My Dearest Evan,

I prayed that this unpleasant task would pass me by, my dear nephew, but I am obliged to inform you that both your mother and father have passed away, victims of the dreaded flu epidemic that is sweeping the country.

I know that you're recovering from serious wounds received in France and that my cruel words will inflict even more pain upon you that you do not deserve. Your parents passed peacefully in their sleep. Your mother was the first to go. A few hours later, your father followed her into the arms of Jesus. It had always been his wish to be at her side to care for her.

Take some solace in the fact that you had such wonderful parents for all these years. Your home was always a place of harmony and love. Be thankful for that. Your ten-year-old sister, Amie, is staying with us. Do not worry about her, Evan, we'll take good care of her. Just concentrate on getting well.

You have always been in our prayers. May the good Lord comfort you in this time of great sorrow.

1

Forgive me for being the messenger of such tragic news. We love you very much and are so proud of your service.

Love,

Aunt Mildred and Family

Evan carefully placed the letter on the stand beside his hospital bed. He had witnessed death on a grand scale in the trenches of France, and though it horrified him, it was a place where you either kill your enemy or he'll kill you. Death took place on an hourly basis. After the initial shock of the gore and bestiality of violent death on the battlefield, most soldiers were able to deal with the unique experience. Sharing that trauma and supporting each other in its aftermath was the key to facing the reality and still be able to function decisively. The Army collectively called it unit cohesion. It created a lifetime bond of fraternity with every participant, leaving their age of innocence forever on the field of battle.

It was ironic. Now, alone in the Walter Reed Army Hospital, Washington, DC, the bad news arrived in the midst of joyful celebrations that the armistice they had all been praying for was imminent. The guns were silent all across the European continent; their prayers had been answered.

Miss Joleen Carpenter, a civilian orderly, noticed him curled up in a fetal position, weeping. She instantly went to his side. "What's wrong, Sergeant Mundy?"

He ignored her presence. She noted the letter on the table and assumed that he had bad news from home. She gently wiped the sweat beads from his forehead and whispered in his ear: "We are setting up some refreshments in the recreation room if you want to celebrate the good news about the war. We just received official confirmation. The Germans have surrendered to the Allies."

He shook his head, "Please, leave me alone."

Miss Carpenter gently patted him on the arm and left him to grieve in private. The noise from the recreation room filtered into the wards. Now every wounded veteran in the hospital could look to the future with certainty. The plans they had placed on hold could now be revisited. Those with the most grievous wounds at least could feel that their sacrifice was worthwhile. The killing had ended, and a great sense of dread and fear was lifted from their shoulders.

Evan was thankful for the news. It helped ease some pain, but his heart was back home in Maine where he grew to manhood. It was difficult for him to imagine life without his mother or father. Their loss was so sudden and unexpected that it left him in a state of dismay and shock. Poor little Amie had to be traumatized by the loss! Just the thought of her needing him at this pivotal time in her life helped to push the sadness to one side and concentrate about the immediate future. He had no doubt that Amie was in good hands with Aunt Mildred and Uncle Dell, but he was determined to seek his release from the hospital as soon as possible.

Once Evan was alone, he stretched out on his cot and stared at the ceiling, remembering what had taken place since he warmly embraced his parents and Amie a year and half ago on his last furlough home before being shipped off to France. It had been a happy occasion as he had anticipated. His precious mother could not contain her tears. It was a heartfelt and teary-eyed parting.

His father had been the last to hold him in his strong arms. He knew first-hand what his son was up against. He had injured his left leg in the war with Cuba several years ago. Evan and his father were very close. They shared similar temperaments, a calm and positive outlook, and were the best of friends.

His father had embraced him for a long time. "We're proud of you, Son. Your sergeant stripes indicate that others also have faith in you. Always be worthy of that trust, and you'll do well. Never forget that your family is anxiously waiting for your safe return home. Good-bye, Son."

"I'll see you all soon, Dad," he had replied soberly.

Over the past eventful months Evan recalled that short conversation with his father. Now, a rush of sadness enveloped him. That promise would not be kept. He questioned why God had taken them home before he had a chance to say good-bye and tell them how much he truly loved and respected them.

The war in France was something he wanted to forget and place behind him. It was a time when fear of being wounded and left to die alone permeated every thought and action. Nations were bent on tearing each other apart regardless of the cost. Once he and his platoon captured seven German prisoners and escorted them to the rear of the front lines. It took a couple of days. In that time he realized that the German soldiers were just like the Americans and British — frightened, cold, hungry and filled with dread of what may be ahead for them. They also had that one-thousand-yard-stare familiar to all combatants regardless of nationality. Evan even felt a certain camaraderie with them by the time they handed them over to Intelligence Headquarters.

His wounds came in September on the main road leading to Paris. The powerful German army was making a thrust aimed at Paris. The French and British were unable to contain the massive effort. The Americans, still unbloodied and untested, were determined to stop the enemy. It was a vicious and costly battle, but the cocky Americans held their ground and eventually pushed the Germans back. Evan's platoon was at the tip of the army's spear poised at the heart of the German effort. He was hit by German machine guns. The bullets that pierced his body felt like red-hot irons that momentarily lifted him off his feet. He fell in the glue-like mud where his blood mixed with the quagmire around him.

Eight bullets penetrated his body. Two each hit his left arm and right leg without serious damage to the bones. The other four bullets had entered his body cavity, destroying his spleen and fracturing several ribs. One bullet had nicked a small portion of his lungs, but he was lucky; none of the bullets hit any vital spots. His recovery would be complete. He had been moved to several hospital locations in France before coming to the United States.

His arm was still in a sling with a small cast, but he was able to use it without the sling. His leg had already healed without complication. The staff at the hospital told him that he would soon be able to leave on an extended visit. His body cavity still hurt and was heavily bandaged in gauze. Nothing

4

could be done for his broken ribs. They would continue to hurt until they had healed. He only had to maintain the tightly covered bandages and refrain from making extreme body movements while they healed themselves. The sudden bad news triggered a renewed desire to be sent home.

The next day, he motioned for Miss Carpenter. She approached him and casually asked, "How are you doing, Sergeant?" There was something different about her this morning. She seemed detached and uncharacteristically sober. Normally her demeanor was bubbly and positive.

Evan studied her carefully and replied, "I'm getting along, Miss Carpenter. I've been thinking about going home. The war is over and I assume that I'll be discharged soon. My wounds have healed enough so that I can travel without discomfort. What do you think?"

She was a rich source of information for the wounded men. It was not uncommon for them to request things from her as if she was a part of the staff instead of a volunteer worker. She avoided Evan's penetrating look and busied herself taking his pulse and sticking a thermometer in his mouth. "The staff may authorize short-term trips from the hospital. Your temp and pulse are normal. I'll ask the staff about a release. It will probably do you some good. Your color is better than yesterday, Sergeant."

"I'll talk about it with the doctors on their morning rounds. Thanks, Miss Carpenter. You've been a lot of help to me and the rest of the patients."

"I'll see you again before I leave the hospital," she told him. There was a nervous twitch in her eye that was unsettling, and he did not know what to make of it.

A little later in the morning, Evan received a letter from his parent's bank in Guilford, Maine, making him aware that there was an outstanding balance of $1,100.00 currently due on the house mortgage. The shock of the notice overrode his grief. He simply did not have that kind of money. His wallet contained about ninety dollars, the full extent of his monetary worth. He did not own an automobile or a horse. He reread the letter and dropped it on the night stand. The bank was asking for the full amount within sixty days. He could not possibly meet their demand. Perhaps they could re-mortgage so that he could make monthly payments, but his salary of ninety dollars barely took care of personal needs. He was not physically capable of holding any demanding job until his wounds completely healed. Evan leaned back against his pillow and thought about his quandary.

Miss Carpenter returned to his ward as she had promised earlier. She noticed his apprehensive mood and asked, "What's wrong, Sergeant?"

He turned to her, shaking his head. "Oh, I'm all right, just a bad day." He was unwilling to give her any more details about his problems at home.

"I wanted to talk to you," she announced in a serious tone. She was nervous and ill at ease. Her dark brown eyes avoided his intense stare. "Why don't we go out on the patio where we can be more private?"

"Sure, if that's what you want."

She knew more about his wounds than he did and was aware that he was capable of walking unaided for short distances. He still used a wheelchair because it was easy to get around and provided a place for him to sit and rest. She wheeled a chair next to the bed for him. Dressed in a pair of pajamas and an Army robe he quickly climbed into the chair and rolled himself toward the large patio at the western end of the hospital.

The sun was beginning to set, covering the distant mountain peaks with a blue haze. Evan thought that the Blue Ridge Mountains lived up to their colorful name. It was a beautiful vista that instantly relaxed him. Sometimes the period between total darkness and daylight highlighted portions of the landscape that had been invisible a short time before or after. Evan remained silent a few moments, enjoying the tranquility and peacefulness of the pastoral scene.

He turned the wheelchair toward Joleen Carpenter and was shocked; she was on the verge of tears. "Now I can ask you what's wrong, Miss Carpenter? Have I done something that has given you grief?"

She leaned against the heavy granite rails of the patio and looked away. She shook her head in dismay, turning to confront him with a resolute expression. "No, you haven't given me any grief, Sergeant Mundy. My reason for being so mysterious is to ask something of you that is very painful to me."

"Is it something about me?" he asked, getting out of the chair to lean against the granite rail beside her.

She shook her head. "It has nothing to do with you, Sergeant, and everything to do with a very serious and delicate situation in my family. Before I continue, may I ask you a few questions first?"

"Sure," he replied, feeling a little awkward about her erratic behavior.

"You're in a ward where I have been pleased to be able to help those who needed it. Our platonic relationship has been very pleasant and free of controversy."

He shook his head in agreement.

"Please don't be shocked, but have you ever entertained any feelings of wanting to know me better?"

The question cut through him like a knife, for everybody in the ward was probably in love with her. She brought a ray of sunshine and hope into their lives by being the kind, thoughtful and considerate person that she was.

"I can't deny having such thoughts, Miss Carpenter. I'm not alone in that respect as you must well know."

"Yes, and I understand the phenomenon, it's part of the healing process," she exclaimed, nervously searching for the right words. "Sergeant Mundy, would you be offended if I asked you to personally do something for me over the next several days away from the hospital?"

He hesitated to answer, noting her discomfort. "Miss Carpenter, under certain circumstances, I'd be flattered to spend some time with you. What do you have in mind?"

Now she became even more unstrung and began to stutter. "No, no, I do not mean like on a date. Listen, I know that I'm sounding strange. Please allow me to explain. I want you to accompany me on a yacht here in Washington on the Potomac River for the next few days. And I want you to pose as my husband…"

"Your husband?" he cried in disbelief.

"Yes, as my husband. Please let me finish. This is very painful for me. You're strong enough to be granted a few days release from the hospital. I've already checked with the staff.

I'm prepared to pay you two thousand dollars for you to act as my husband in the company of my mother and father," she was breathing heavily now. "I know that this is an unusual request, and before you answer, there is more. At the end of the few days, maybe four, you may return to the ward and never, I repeat emphatically, never repeat to another soul what took place during that period. I will demand that you give your word to remain silent. If you cannot grant me that assurance, then we must simply forget this conversation. Think it over, Sergeant. I'll return after I check on a few things in the upstairs ward. Please do not badger me with questions I cannot answer. The money will be paid in cash. One thousand dollars the day we start this adventure, and the other thousand after we part company, and you are released from your commitment."

The proposal Joleen Carpenter had just made to him was the most bizarre thing he had ever encountered. It was most uncharacteristic of the friendly aide who had consistently projected a picture of wholesomeness and selflessness that everyone in the ward admired. He was at a complete loss as to what his answer would be, watching her walk off the patio. If anyone had suggested that she was capable of planning and executing the plan she had proposed to him, no one would believe it.

His first impulse was to refuse the proposition. It was a strange coincidence that she offered him two thousand dollars for a few days of his time on the same day he received notice of the mortgage coming due. It would take him years to accumulate that much money. The more he thought about it, the more interested he became. The monetary part of the plan interested him, but it made him feel greedy.

When Miss Carpenter returned, she had an apprehensive look on her face. "I've come to see if you've given my proposal any thought. I understand how strange it must sound to you. I can't answer the many questions you must have. My happiness and that of my family depend on a successful performance of my plan. The very generous amount of money is offered because you might not accept for less."

Evan looked at the lines around her face and the determined tilt of her chin. "Is it really that important to you?"

8

"Oh yes," she sighed in a low voice.

"Why me? Why not someone else?" he asked.

"I cannot tell you why," she answered defiantly. "You must be prepared to do whatever I ask you to do without questioning the reason why."

"Is this something illegal that could get me into trouble with the law?" he asked pointedly. "If so, you've got the wrong boy, Miss Carpenter."

"I would never ask you to do something that is harmful to you or anyone else. When our adventure is over, we simply go on with our lives as if it never took place. I must caution you again there must be complete secrecy. The money is offered to maintain your silence as much as it is to be an actor in a play. Now, have you arrived at a decision?"

"To say that I'm uncomfortable with the arrangement is a gross understatement. I can use the money for good purpose back home; therefore, I accept your proposal and the conditions you have outlined," Evan told her. "However, on a lighter note, if the guys in the ward knew that I was to pose as your husband, most of them would be green with envy."

"Sergeant Mundy," she smiled with him. "You overestimate my popularity with the other soldiers."

Chapter Two

That night, Evan stared at the ceiling wondering about the strange proposal he had just accepted. The money could be put to good use for little Amie and himself. He was uncomfortable with the arrangement, but more good could come out of the deal than the anxiety he would have to go through to execute it.

Later that evening, Evan received a letter from Roberta Gibson, a good friend and classmate since they went to first grade together.

Dear Evan,

This past week I've been so consumed with grief I don't know where to turn. The flu has devastated this town and just might have destroyed our family, too. Both our parents died within a week of each other. I'm not sure if Bob and I can keep the farm going. Bob was severely weakened by his gas exposure in France.

You must think I'm selfish. Here I am doing nothing but complain to you who has had to suffer the same news in a distant Army hospital recovering from war wounds. My heart goes out to you, dear friend. Know that you are always in my prayers and thoughts. I think often of our days in school. I was always proud to call you my friend. Those occasions when you played the violin and I sang will always be the most precious memories for me.

I stopped by your Aunt Mildred's house to see Amie yesterday. She seemed lost. All we can do is to be there for her and to let her know that her welfare is our main concern. She's so proud of you and is anxious for you to come home. She needs you, Evan, more than you know. She worries a lot about the seriousness of your wounds and is afraid that you, too, will leave her alone.

All of us are looking forward to the day when you will be well enough to come home. Bob sends his best and, of course, I do the same.

Love,

Roberta

Evan placed the letter on the stand and fell back against the pillow, remembering how it had been. Bob and Roberta were his best friends in the small town of Monson on the edge of the great Maine woods. The Gibsons lived a few miles from the village on the same road as the Mundy family. The two families were not only neighbors, but good friends. Bob was a tall muscular Finn with blond hair and blue eyes, a serious young man who had always worked hard on the small family dairy farm. Bob and Evan often went hunting and fishing together.

Roberta also had blond hair, frequently wearing it in a single braid down the middle of her shoulders. She was small-boned with finely chiseled facial features that made her look older than she actually was. She had an out-going personality, contrasting with Bob's modest ways. She was a soprano, and even as a young girl she had a remarkable ability to sing most any type of song. She liked some of the classical pieces but really preferred the Scotch-Irish folk tunes her mother played on a violin brought from Prince Edward Island.

Evan could easily recall the day he had sat on the Gibson's front porch when he was seven or eight years old. Mrs. Gibson was playing *An Irish Lullaby* on the violin in her parlor. The soothing music had touched a nerve with him and he was determined to learn to play the instrument. A few days later, he had nervously asked Mrs. Gibson if she could teach him how to play. She was a matronly lady who wore her dark hair in a bun at the back of her head, and always seemed to be wearing an apron.

She observed young Evan and wrapped her arms affectionately around him. "My dear Evan, I will be glad to teach you what I can, but first, you need an instrument and a bow. Do you have a violin at home?"

"No, Mrs. Gibson," he had replied, disappointed, because there was no extra money to buy one. "I'd be willing to work for one."

She had smiled at him and told him, "You should have your mother teach you to read music and possibly some basic stuff on the piano. Later, when you've earned some money, maybe we can find a used instrument for you to purchase. In the meantime, we'll keep our eyes and ears peeled for a good violin."

From that moment, Evan became an avid student of music. His parents were in agreement with Mrs. Gibson's suggestion. He never forgot his tenth birthday. His mother and father had located a fine instrument that an elderly man in town was offering for sale.

The price was two cords of firewood cut and split. He had helped his father cut the wood in their woodlot. Some of the wood was too large to handle easily, so his father had split the pieces open with black powder. He remembered that working around the wood always gave him a headache. They delivered the firewood by making three trips through the village on the snow-covered roads with their large yarding sled drawn by their powerful Belgian draft horse. Evan had a great sense of achievement after they had delivered and piled the last load of wood.

The owner of the violin was a large man with a beard and a French accent. The kids in town called him Joe Frenchman. Evan never knew his real name until years later — Joseph Bolduc. Bringing that violin home was one of the happiest days of his life. His father was proud of how hard he had worked to get the instrument. It was a beautiful violin with good tone.

The country was at war. He had already signed up for the Army and was scheduled to leave two days after graduation along with several others from town, including Bob. The last day of school in his senior year, Roberta had sung several songs at their graduation ceremonies in the town hall. He had accompanied her with his violin. The Town had a small group of musicians that had formed an orchestra. His mother played the piano; there was an elderly man who played the drums; and Mrs. Gibson played the violin. Occasionally, Evan sat in with them. The orchestra softly played background accompaniment while Evan took the lead with Roberta.

Roberta had selected to do *Londonderry Aire* as her final selection. She had turned to Evan who always positioned himself slightly to her left and one step to the rear. "This one is just for you, Evan."

He had blushed briefly and raised the violin to his shoulder, playing a brief introduction for her to begin. For that song, the rest of the ensemble on stage remained quiet. The music touched the hearts of everyone present, bringing tears to some eyes. Roberta had the gift of giving heart and soul to any song she sang, but that night, she created an emotional experience that the people still talked about. Evan had also contributed to the event, following her clear soprano voice to the high notes with a soft ringing tone that brought tears to Roberta's eyes. They were spiritually and emotionally a part of the music. Her voice vibrated through the small town hall. The audience was mesmerized, fully aware that they were experiencing something unique in their small community.

Roberta ended the ballad with the soft refrain: *Oh Danny Boy, Oh Danny Boy, I Love You So.* Evan held the last few notes slowly using the full length of the bow. The audience was silent for a moment, still held by the power of the performance they had just witnessed. When he removed the violin from his shoulder, the hall erupted in applause. Roberta curtsied to them and turned to Evan. Their eyes met, both aware that something special had just taken place. She stepped into his arms and kissed him. The audience continued to applaud.

Evan recalled that magical event with distinct clarity. It was the moment of discovery — he was in love with Roberta, and she loved him in return. How he yearned to see her again. Thoughts of her had sustained him when he was cold, frightened and filled with anxiety about how he handled the squads of infantrymen in his charge.

Incessant artillery barrages obliterated everything above ground. The fields and forests were plowed into pulverized black ooze that clung to their bodies like glue. Mazes of churned trenches were often the final graves of whole companies of men when they took a direct hit. The fetid trenches wreaked with urine and feces mixed with the pungent scent of cordite and gunpowder. He knew what it was like to be so frightened that rational thinking was impossible. The conditions the men had to endure contrasted to the life-sustaining memories of clean sheets on a bed, sweet-smelling roses on the table for a Sunday dinner, and perfumed women. The thought of someone who loved you waiting for your return fueled the fires of hope and great expectations. Those who could not connect with warm memories of the past were destined to experience the full terror of the battlefield. Many became casualties and never recovered from the trauma, destined to relive the horror over and over again.

In that debilitating atmosphere, the memory of Roberta smiling at him brought a calm moment of escape to his troubled soul. Without her, he was convinced that he would never have survived the crucible of terror that tested every man's limit to endure. His remembrances were interrupted by a soft voice calling to him in the dark ward.

"Sergeant Mundy."

He turned to see Joleen Carpenter standing beside him. "Yes, I'm awake. Old memories are sweet to recall."

"I'm sure they are," she replied, placing a clipboard at the foot of his bed. "I've spoken to the doctors, and they all agree that an outing of a few days would be good for you. Are you prepared to fulfill my request?"

He was anxious to get this commitment over with. "Yes. If it wasn't such a lucrative thing, I'd decline. The fact that I'm willingly doing something I instinctively don't want to do makes me feel cheap and greedy."

"Try to push those kinds of thoughts out of your mind, Sergeant. Sure, what I've asked you to do is deception, but it is done to serve a greater good. Trust me, please."

"I'm willing to do my part," he replied.

"Will you be emotionally and physically prepared to begin our operation tomorrow midday?"

"The sooner the better for me."

She seemed more nervous than Evan about the project. "I don't want to brief you here in the hospital. As soon as I obtain your release, we'll go to a secluded location where I'll fill you in on all you need to know. I'm sorry if it all seems so mysterious. The hardest thing for the both of us will be to act like newlyweds, when in reality, we are strangers. Let's try to help each other without overdoing it in the affection department. Do you understand?" The fact that she was uncomfortable with the arrangement put him more at ease.

The next morning, he went through some intense checkups. All of the doctors were willing to release him in Joleen Carpenter's care. He was capable of walking unaided for short distances. His strength was increasing each day. He had made up his mind to accept the expedition as a fun lark with no responsibility for his actions or lack of them. She was completely in control, and he was resolved to play his part with all the skill he was capable of delivering to the situation.

They left the hospital in a taxicab that took them into Washington where Joleen pointed out the Capitol Building and the Mall. They traveled down Pennsylvania Avenue across the Anacostia River where they took a sharp right following the river to an isolated park on the east bank. It was an attractive overview at the juncture of the Potomac River and Anacostia River.

She told the driver to wait for them. They left the vehicle and took a bench seat facing the rivers. She had brought a thermos of coffee and offered him some. He gladly accepted her thoughtfulness.

"From now on, I'm going to call you Evan instead of Sergeant Mundy. You should call me Joleen whenever you address me. Other terms of endearment may be appropriate at times; you must decide that on your own.

"My mother, father, and oldest sister, Aline, who is caring for the one-month-old baby boy, Alex, are already on my father's yacht. Now, as far as my family knows, you and I have been friends since you were stationed at Fort Belvoir prior to going overseas. We got married February 2, 1918 in Alexandria, Virginia. Remember Alex, the name of our baby boy. It is at the heart of this adventure."

Evan listened in silence. So far he believed he could play the role as long as the family did not pick him apart with questions. "How do you know your family will not check on our marriage certificate?"

"Oh, yes, I have two gold wedding bands, one for each of us." She smiled and handed him the ring, to place on his

15

finger. "I'll bet you never thought you'd get married so quickly, eh?"

He was relieved that she was able to smile. "Thanks."

"Now, be assured that no one will be asking for our marriage certificate or anything like that. The family knows that you and I are married. I've described you to them, so try to be your natural self, and you'll be fine."

"Any father that loves his daughter as yours must, has to be interested in how her husband is going to provide for her. I have no job, and I've been in the Army for two years. What do I tell them when they ask me what am I going to do for work? I'm not rich. On the contrary, I'm a simple country farm boy with not much going for me. Your father would want better than that for his daughter."

"Your concern is valid, Evan, so tell me what are you planning to do when you go home? I ask only because we should be on the same page with that story."

She had turned to look into his eyes. He saw his reflection in her brown eyes and knew that he should be careful. This very lovely lady would be easy to love and be with every day. He was only a paid servant, and he should not forget that important fact of life!

"I'd tell them that I want to go to college after the Army to study forestry. I'd work all I could to provide the necessities for my family. In the meantime, I will own the farm which can provide a lot of our needs. The house is clear and free of a mortgage. If it becomes a necessity, we could borrow money against the property," he told her. "Of course, the money you give me will make it possible for me to own the property. That's the main reason I'm doing this for you, Joleen."

"That sounds great to me. My mother and father are very practical people. They have been financially successful and I do not want you to feel inferior or unworthy in any way," she was quick to explain.

"My experience in France gave me an insight into what is important in life. Believe me, I do not rate people by the size of their bank account which has nothing to do with the human virtues which have defined humanity for centuries. By the way, do you want me to embrace and kiss you in front of your parents?"

"Perhaps, if it is natural and spontaneous. After all, we're almost newlyweds," she answered, avoiding his searching eyes.

He nodded his head in agreement. "One other question I have to ask. Do we sleep together?"

She blushed at the question, a good indication that it was a subject that needed to be discussed. "The baby will sleep with me in a small stateroom. You'll be in an adjoining room. Separate beds and rooms because the baby may wake up crying and need to be fed or have his diapers changed. The doors will remain unlocked, so I'm placing you on your honor to stay in your room during the night. Do not misunderstand me, Evan Mundy, I do not intend to prostitute myself for this venture. Do I make my position clear?"

"It is what I would expect from you, Joleen. I promise to respect your request."

"Do you have any other questions before we board the yacht?" she asked.

"I'm sure there will be some as we progress through the days. I think you've touched on most everything I need to know," he replied hesitantly. "A condition has crossed my mind during this past hour we've been together. When this is over, you mention that we go back to our old routines and forget the episode. What if we find during this strange interlude that we're attracted to each other? Do you have someone 'special' in your life? What if I fall in love with you? Do you expect me to simply walk away and not look back as if nothing happened? People have feelings, you know…?"

She avoided his eyes. "To be perfectly honest, I never entertained such a thing. I was considering a sterile impersonal act, free of emotions, and I urge you to not dwell on any other possibility. It would destroy everything I'm trying to accomplish."

"Just what are you trying to accomplish, Joleen?"

"I cannot answer that question!"

Chapter Three

Two days later, Evan was standing on the forward deck of a small yacht as it plowed a furrow through the dark blue waters of the Atlantic on an azimuth slightly south of due east. They were off Cape Hatteras, a third of the distance to Bermuda. A Coast Guard cutter came up beside them and with a friendly toot of its horn, sped northward leaving a heavy wake behind.

He was mesmerized by the intensity and magnitude of the brilliant orange-red sunset at sea. It was the most colorful experience he had ever witnessed. Without realizing it, Joleen came to stand beside him. She had seen similar scenes before from the same ship, but tonight, it was as if she was seeing it for the first time.

He turned to her and said, "This is one scene I'll always remember."

She had discovered that Sergeant Mundy was a young man of many moods. He was not educated by standards her family was accustomed to, but he was courteous, respectful, and even after experiencing the horrors of trench-warfare, he still maintained an innocence and an integrity that was refreshing. She found him sincere and honest, and felt guilty that she had talked him into a situation that required duplicity with a smile.

"I want to thank you for making this so easy, Evan. My sister Aline is with the baby now. Since you've had a chance to spend some time with my mother and father, what do you think of them?"

He continued to stare at the sunset, carefully choosing his words. "I have to tell you that they are nothing like I expected. Your mother is lovely like her two daughters. The three of you look alike. Your mother is younger than I anticipated. She has an air about her that at first glance could be interpreted as

18

haughty and superior. Possibly she projects that persona to hide some nervous insecurities. She's polite and proper — I think that's the correct word. I'm still not sure if she's sincere in the way she praises our marriage. She has a hard time making eye contact with me. Perhaps she's still trying to evaluate me, which would not be unusual for a mother."

"What about my father?" she asked, taking his arm, and leading him to two recliner chairs on the deck.

"I found your mother an enigma. Now your father is a man much like my very own father. He's sincere and straightforward in his speech and actions. I'm betting that he made his fortune the hard way by working for it. He just doesn't strike me as the typical corporate tycoon type. He gives credit to others for his success and appears to be a very generous man to those whom he judges to be worthy. He has never made me feel inferior or 'measuring up' to the standards your society frequently imposes on people. I like him and feel bad that I'm deceiving the man. I think he deserves better.

"Your father seems older than your mother, but that may be the result of polio. When you told me that he was confined to a wheel- chair, I expected to see a bitter and angry man. Instead, he smiles often and seems to enjoy life. I hope that I have that kind of courage."

She had asked, and he had honestly told her what he thought. Not once had he tried to take advantage of the situation. He was a modest country boy and a little shy. The first time he held her hand and lightly kissed her, she saw him blush. It made her feel comfortable with him, and that had to relate to a better performance in the play they were acting out.

The next day, Evan fished off the stern of the yacht, catching enough cod and mackerel to feed the crew and guests for one meal. He wanted to try his luck at skeet shooting, but Joleen and her father talked him out of it. The heavy kick from the twelve gauge shotgun could irritate his broken ribs and shoulder, so he conceded to their request.

The last evening of their cruise, Evan played cribbage with Mr. Carpenter in his private study, a large room in the center of the vessel filled with books of every description. They played several hands with Evan winning two out of four hands. He was attracted to a violin case on a shelf.

"Is that your violin, Mr. Carpenter?"

The elder Lamont Carpenter looked longingly at the case. "Yes, Evan, it's mine. I haven't been able to play for several years. It's one of those things I miss the most."

"May I try it out, Sir?" Evan had not played for almost two years.

"I didn't know you played the violin. Sure, give it a try. You'll have to tune it. I had always hoped that one of the girls would take it up, but they never seemed interested."

Evan placed the case on the table, removing the instrument and the bow. It was a Gottlieb, manufactured in Germany. He plucked each string and adjusted them by ear. They were only slightly out of tune. "My, what a beautiful violin. The tone is superb." Anxious to try it out, he went up and down the scale several times before he commenced his all-time favorite, *LONDONDERRY AIRE.*

Lamont Carpenter watched his young son-in-law for a few moments and closed his eyes, listening closely to the light touch that Evan brought to the instrument. When the selection was completed, he exclaimed with enthusiasm, "Bravo, my son, bravo. You have made my day. Where did you learn to play like that?"

"Well, my mother helped me a lot. She played the piano very well. A dear friend and neighbor gave me several lessons once we were able to purchase a used violin. Music has always been a big part of my family. I've missed it since I joined the Army."

Lamont Carpenter smiled at him. "I enjoyed your rendition of that old Irish favorite. What a nice way to end the day. I'm getting a little tired. Would you please roll me back to my stateroom? Please use the violin as much as you want. I hate to see this short time with you end. It's been special for me. Joleen has chosen well."

The compliment was graciously received by Evan. To have won this gentle man's respect was important to him. "I, too, am glad that we could meet, Sir. I didn't quite know what to expect when we began this trip out to sea. Thank you for receiving me the way you have. I'll be glad to roll you back to your room."

Joleen met them as they were leaving the study. She had seen how Evan and her father had interacted and was pleased. She paid more attention to her father than her sister, Aline, or her mother. He had the feeling that they were not a close or supporting family; they simply lived together. Joleen and Evan helped the feeble man from the wheel chair to his bed. He was pale and weak. Joleen seemed to be earnestly concerned about him, and was quiet as they left his stateroom.

"He's not doing very well, is he, Joleen?" Evan asked in a hushed voice.

"He has failed some since we left Washington," she remarked. "I did notice that his color was better and his spirits were higher when he was playing cribbage with you, Evan."

"Your father's a good man. I really like him. I think we could become good friends given the chance," he replied, watching her reaction.

"I believe you, Evan. We all heard you playing the violin. You were very good," she told him, taking a seat at the stern of the vessel. They were traveling faster than usual leaving a large wake in their trail. "We'll be heading into the Potomac soon. I plan to leave the ship tomorrow. My father will be returning to the care facility where my mother placed him. He's quite comfortable there where they can monitor his condition."

"Then tomorrow our understanding comes to an end."

"Yes," she replied in a strained voice. "This has not been an easy voyage for me, and you do not have to know why. However, I do want to thank you and tell you that I've appreciated your kind and considerate ways. You've made an unbearable situation more tolerable. I thank you for that."

"It has been an interesting diversion for me. I feel sorry for your father and wish him well. I've had a chance to watch you function under difficult conditions, and I admire your loyalty to your family. Under normal circumstances you and I would never travel in the same social circles. It has been nice being with you, and I can honestly confess that I'll miss the few moments we've spent together on this excursion. Having said that, I believe I'll turn in also. I'm weary, too. Goodnight, Mrs. Mundy." He bent down to kiss her.

She lifted her lips to his. "Goodnight, Evan. Rest well."

That next morning, the yacht tied up at the Washington Navy Yard dock. The small crew secured the ship and lowered the gangplank. Lamont Carpenter was the first to leave the ship. He was assisted down the gangplank and placed in a waiting limousine. Evan and Joleen watched him and waved from the main deck.

Joleen went with Evan to get their luggage. They said good-bye to Aline and Mrs. Carpenter who was cradling the baby in her arms. Joleen promised to return after she deposited him in the hospital. He waved to the two women at the rail and entered the taxicab. On their way to the hospital, Joleen placed an envelope in his hands.

"This is your payment as promised, Evan. You certainly deserve every penny. Thank you so much. Now, I must repeat the conditions we agreed on. What you saw or heard these past few days are never to be divulged or spoken about. Your silence is important."

"You don't have to worry about me, Joleen. Thanks for the money. It'll help me a lot and allow me to take care of my younger sister who needs me." He turned to look into her eyes. "Is this the end for us?"

"You know it is, Evan. Don't ask me why, I can't tell you. I'm going to spend some time with my father, so I won't be visiting the wards for a while. You may be gone by then. I wish you and Amie all the best."

"Can we write to each other?"

She shook her head and smiled. "No, it's for the best that we go our separate ways and pick up the threads of our lives. Having said that, you'll always be a special friend who shared and helped me at a difficult time in my life."

The cab stopped at the entrance to the hospital. Evan had only a small duffel bag and wanted to handle it by himself. "Good-bye, Joleen. I wish you all the best. It's been swell being with you."

He leaned over to kiss her one last time. She returned the caress. "Good-bye, friend."

"Good-bye..." He walked slowly into the hospital without looking back.

Evan eagerly sought the comfort of his familiar hospital bed in the ward. He was weary and needed some quiet space to put the past few days into perspective. On his table were two letters. One from Amie and one from an insurance agency in Guilford, Maine. He quickly opened the latter and was amazed to learn that, years ago, his parents had taken out an insurance policy on their lives. Ten thousand dollars was available for him at the agency. The unexpected gift from two loving parents brought tears to his eyes. Even in death, they were showing their love and concern for their two children.

A ward nurse saw him staring at the ceiling and came to his bedside. "Is something wrong, Sergeant?" She had spoken softly and asked again, "Are you all right, Sergeant Mundy?"

He opened his eyes and saw her. "Yes, I'm okay. Memories from home, that's all."

"You are not on the list for dinner. Do you want me to get you something to eat?"

"That would be nice, nurse. I'll just have the soup of the day."

"I'll be right back."

Evan sat up to read the letter from Amie. Her handwriting brought a smile to his lips. He was anxious to get home so that he could comfort her. She was too young and innocent to be burdened with the sorrows she had to bear alone.

Monson, Maine
November 8, 1918

Dear Evan,

Aunt Mildred has gone shopping for a few groceries. She sends you her love and we all pray for you to get well soon. My school teacher, Mrs. Pennington, told me that you were once her pupil in the fourth grade. Everyone is worried for you, Evan. I'm looking forward to the day you can come home. Aunt Mildred and Uncle Dell are wonderful to me and I love them very much, but I'm anxious to go back home in my own room.

Robert Gibson hauled a supply of firewood to our house for this coming heating season. He's nice. He spent some time with me telling me how his parents, Mother, and Father are all together in Heaven the same as they were here on earth. I understand that, but it still hurts a lot and I miss them so much.

23

Uncle Dell has just finished piling a supply of firewood for the kitchen stove in the shed. I helped him with it. The nights are getting colder and a fire feels good.

This letter comes to you, big Brother, with lots of love. I'm so proud of you. I keep a picture of you in uniform on my bed stand. You're very handsome.

Goodnight, Brother,

Love, Amie

He read the letter a second time while eating his soup. The nurse who brought him a hot cup of coffee and a fresh piece of apple pie had mentioned that Joleen Carpenter was resigning her volunteer work at the hospital. That surprised him. He thought she was only taking a few days off to be with her father. He spent a sleepless night thinking about her. When the sun rose out of the east above the surrounding trees, Evan was still unable to define the illusive lady!

Several days after his return to the Walter Reed Hospital, Evan received word that he could go home. He had been given extensive tests and examinations, and felt stronger each day. He was to remain in the Army until his wounds completely healed. He received suitable uniforms for the Maine winter conditions from the quartermaster and was informed that he was to report to the nearest Army or National Guard facility for further evaluations and eventual discharge from the Army.

Leaving some of his buddies in the ward was difficult. They had been a constant source of support and encouragement for the future. Regardless of their grievous wounds, an air of hope permeated the wards. A long-standing bond of fellowship had been established that time could not erase. They were a unique and select brotherhood of warriors, and he would miss their friendship.

He took a train from Washington, D.C., to Portland, Maine, where he boarded a Canadian Pacific train to Greenville. He stepped off the train in Greenville, two days later, happy to be back in familiar surroundings. The sweet smell of spruce and fir forests reminded him that he had truly come back home where he belonged. He had often thought that he would never see home again. Within a couple of hours, a local Hasey Maine Stage coach left Greenville taking him to the small village of Monson. He had the driver drop him off at the road leading to their home south of the village proper.

He was returning home from a war that left him weaker than he was when he left. He had seen enough of war and its brutalities. He thought of Amie and of Roberta, and his heart beat faster. No joy is greater than the homecoming of a warrior who survived the crucibles of combat!

Chapter Four

How strange it was for Evan to be returning home to his beloved Maine. He had traveled halfway across the country to Georgia where he took basic training in the Army. Then he left for France, crossing the dark Atlantic where his preconceived notions of combat were permanently shattered. He had left home a young man prepared to take on the world. He was returning an older individual, burdened with ugly memories that might never set him free. Still, the brisk air and clean smell of the northern forests filled him with thanksgiving and hope for the future. This was where his roots were, and, now, his parents were buried in its soil.

Evan had visions of his mother and father on that last day of his short furlough home before being shipped overseas. His mother had been unable to contain her grief and wept openly, holding him close in a tight embrace. His father had valiantly held back the tears, but a firm set to his jaw told Evan that it was a difficult parting. He always knew that he was loved. That parting simply reinforced his belief.

The short walk down the road to his home was filled with memories of days past. The sun was just beginning to set behind the western mountains as he passed the Gibson home. He looked to see if anyone was around. A single light shone in the kitchen. His heart beat faster, hoping that Roberta would be somewhere in sight. Disappointed, he continued on for another five minutes to his childhood home. Sight of the white New England style home with the heavily pitched roof brought a sigh to his lips.

It was getting dark, yet he could see that the fields had been mowed by the neighbors. Amie had written to tell him that the two horses belonging to his parents were being cared for at the Gibson farm. He turned into the long driveway and had trouble holding back the tears bursting to be free. He

26

unlocked the front door and let himself into the front parlor off the porch facing the road. His parents had electricity installed right after he left for basic training. He reached for the light switch to his left and turned on the lights.

Setting his duffel down on the floor, Evan scanned the room through misty eyes, remembering how he had loved the evening hours when all of the family were in the room. It had been his favorite time of day after his parents had completed their chores. The balance of the day was devoted to the family.

Stepping into the kitchen off the parlor, he saw that the woodbox was filled with dry hardwood and some spruce kindling wood to ignite a fire. Shortly he had a fire going in the cast iron kitchen cook stove. He primed the pump beside the sink with a tumbler of water and drew a teapot of water for a cup of tea. Retrieving a small brick of cheddar cheese, black bread and a small tin of tea from his duffel, he sat at the large oak table in the kitchen waiting for the water to boil. The air was filled with the strong presence of his parents. The house was a powerful reminder of their loss, and he was surprised that he was handling it so well.

When he received the news of their deaths, he had spent sleepless nights grieving their passing. His hope for the future was that he would be strong enough to take care of Amie. The evening hush was pierced by the melancholic calls of whippoorwills from two separate locations around the house. He had often tried to locate them, but was never able to get a live view. It was almost as if they were welcoming him home. Their calls had been a part of his life for as long as he could remember.

That next morning he awoke from a sound sleep in his familiar childhood bed. He planned to get one of the horses from the Gibson's to hitch to the wagon in the barn. His first thought was to bring Amie home, and then do some shopping for supplies. It was blustery out with heavy clouds overhead. The great coat the Army had given him felt good over his uniform. He noted smoke coming from the Gibson's chimney. That meant someone was up.

Roberta had spotted Evan from the kitchen window and ran as fast as she could out the driveway towards him, her blond braid swinging from side to side. The minute he saw her a choking cry passed his lips. She flung herself into his arms and buried her head on his shoulder.

"Oh my dearest Evan. Thank God you're home," she cried with trembling lips. "We've all missed you so much. Thank God, thank God."

He held her close to his heart filled with emotion. "There were many times in France when I was afraid I'd never see you again, Roberta. Holding you is like a dream come true. I didn't stop last night. I simply had to face the reality that Ma and Pa were not home waiting for me. How tragic that you and Bob have had to go through the same thing."

She pulled away and held him at arms length. "You've lost weight, Evan. Those lines around your eyes and mouth give you a stark austere look that is so unlike you. I love you, Evan Mundy." She kissed him on the lips.

"Knowing that you were waiting for me helped more than you'll ever know."

"I'm going to erase all of those ugly images, dear Evan," she cried, tracing the lines on his face. Her soft touch sent tingles through his body.

"Tell me, Roberta. How is Amie doing?"

"I stopped by your Aunt Mildred's to see her yesterday. Considering what she had to go through, she's doing quite well. She's a little more withdrawn than you remember her, and her eyes just break your heart. She really needs you, Evan. She has been paranoid that you, too, were going to leave her. What a happy day this is going to be for her."

He told of his plan to pick up one of the horses and return to the barn to hitch up the wagon. She led him to the stalls in the barn where the gentle mare was eating a ration of oats. Evan asked about Bob and how he was doing recuperating from gas exposure. Roberta told him that he was getting stronger and was working part-time at the Monson Maine Slate Company.

Roberta walked with Evan back to the barn to help him hook up the wagon. "Do you want me to go with you, or do you think it might be best if the two of you work things out without any intrusions?"

"You are not a stranger or an intruder," he scolded.

"I know, but right now you're all she has, and just maybe you need her more than she needs you. I'll see you later when you return."

"Thanks for being here, Roberta," he replied, holding her in a strong embrace. She gently kissed both of his eyes and sent him on his way. The mare trotted all the way back through the village without any directions from Evan. He gently pulled her to the right down the road leading toward one of the slate quarries and pulled her to a stop in front of a yellow house with a large sun porch on the front. He placed a weight to the horse's halter and rushed to the side of the house toward the kitchen entrance.

Amie had just eaten breakfast and was helping her aunt clean up the kitchen when she saw him pass by the window. She let out a scream and ran to the door. Evan stepped inside and swept his sister off her feet in a warm embrace.

"Hi, Amie, I've come to take you home with me."

Aunt Mildred watched the two with tears of thanksgiving running down her cheeks. She was a small, energetic lady with gray hair and pronounced facial features. She had always been an important part of the children's lives. She was very close to their father.

Amie was speechless and desperately clung to Evan. She normally had an outgoing personality with many friends in school, but since the death of her mother and father she had withdrawn to the point that their aunt was concerned about her welfare. She was relieved that Evan had finally come home. Amie's dark brown hair was done up in braids most of the time. She had grown taller since he last saw her.

"Are you ready to come home, Amie?"

Blinded by tears, she looked into his sad eyes. "The memories are so strong back home. It really hurts, Evan. It hurts a lot..."

"I know, Sis, I know. It's the same for me, too, but we have to accept the reality that Ma and Pa are not with us anymore. They still share our every moment from the unique world they are now a part of. When you're sad, they'll be sad with you. Remember how much they loved both of us. That did not change when they died. Let's think of the happy times we all had, and there were many."

Aunt Mildred observed what had passed between them and breathed a sigh of relief. For a brief moment she saw that sparkle in Amie's eyes that had always defined her as a happy child. Evan's return was already working the miracle Amie needed.

Amie encircled his neck with her arms and silently wept in his embrace. "I was so afraid of losing you, too, Evan."

"I know, Sis," he replied. "Come, I'll help you get your things together."

"You're going to need some groceries, Evan," Aunt Mildred suggested. "Your mother had canned several quarts of vegetables and fruits before the fever struck. I'll put together a box of fresh bread Amie and I baked yesterday. We have a full pot of baked beans that needs to be finished off in the oven for an hour or so, too."

Evan released Amie and embraced his aunt. "What would we have done without your help, dear Aunt Mildred? Thank you for being the wonderful person you are. Uncle Dell chose wisely," he smiled at her.

She was pleased to see that Evan still had that soft knack of reaching out to people. His eyes reflected the horrors he had experienced, but she knew that, in time, those memories would soon be overshadowed, never forgotten, but becoming less and less influential in his everyday affairs. Her husband, Dell, had once returned from the war against Spain with the same look. "How proud we've been of you, Evan. I hated to have to write my last letter to you. My, you look nice in your uniform. Your folks would be proud of the sergeant stripes on your arms. Do you have to report back to the Army?"

"My medical discharge will be effective when I report to the nearest Army facility for an evaluation of my wounds. I can get that done at the Greenville or Dexter National Guard Armory," Evan told her.

She left the kitchen to help Amie gather her things. A few minutes later, they returned with a suitcase. Aunt Mildred busied herself placing the beans and bread in a sturdy cardboard box, and looked up at him with a smile. "Amie and I made two apple pies yesterday. This one will fit perfectly in the box. I'll give you a quart of milk, too. It's cold enough to keep it in the woodshed for now."

Evan carried the food box to the wagon and returned for Amie's suitcase. "Thanks for everything, Aunt Mildred," he said, kissing her on the forehead. "How nice it is to be home, where people care for each other. Are you all set, Sis?"

Aunt Mildred saw her smile at him and was content that her niece was going to be fine. "I'm ready, Evan. I wasn't before, but now that you're here, it seems only natural to be going home. Thank you, Aunt Mildred, for everything. I love you and Uncle Dell."

Aunt Mildred waved to them as he turned the wagon around and headed back through the village. They stopped at Hughes store for some groceries and at the post office to check on mail. Several people in town recognized them and wished them well. It gave both of them a warm feeling of belonging to the small northern community. He had a long list of things he wanted to do once he got back home. After shopping and getting the mail, he went to the branch of a Guilford bank located at Hescock's Drug Store to pay the balance due on the house mortgage, and opened a savings account in his and Amie's name.

Upon entering the store he was warmly greeted by Fred Hescock, the pharmacist and owner of the store who treated them to a large chocolate ice cream soda. Evan and Amie sat at one of the small circular tables enjoying the soda. The place brought back fond memories of his youth. Evan shared an event with Amie that remained a benchmark in his life.

It took place about fourteen years ago when he was six years old. He was standing on the sidewalk near the entrance to the drug store, waiting for his father to come into town from the slate quarry where he worked to cash his paycheck and to buy groceries for the week. Young Evan had been eyeing the counter filled with candy just inside the door and had a powerful craving for one of the pieces of hard candy on top of the showcase. Acting on impulse, he quietly went inside when no one was around and took one of the candies, quickly stepping back outside. While he was enjoying the sweet morsel, Mr. Hescock opened the door and motioned him inside.

Evan followed him into the back room where Mr. Hescock made up prescriptions. Evan was scared to death. The kind pharmacist confronted him, letting him know that he had been

31

seen stealing the candy. His ruse had failed! Evan quickly admitted to the deed with a promise that he would never do it again. Mr. Hescock firmly told him that he was disappointed with his conduct, but he would not tell his father if Evan was willing to make restitution for the candy. Evan had quickly agreed to wash and dry several small bottles used for liquid prescriptions, and diligently went about the task while Mr. Hescock left the room to wait on a customer.

Evan finished his chores, proud that he could make up for his misbehavior. When Mr. Hescock returned, he smiled at the thorough job he had done and told him that if he ever had that same urge for a sweet bite to come to him. Frequently the store had broken odds and ends of candy that he would be glad to give to him for nothing. The offer came after a promise to never take anything that was not his to take. Evan had solemnly given his word. He and the kind pharmacist had remained friends throughout the years, sharing a secret that neither divulged to anyone.

"And you, dear little sister," Evan grinned at Amie, enjoying her chocolate soda. "Are the only other person in the world to know about your big brother's illicit behavior as a little boy."

Chapter Five

Amie and Evan were adjusting to their new life without their mother or father. Amie had a longer walk to get to school than when she was at Aunt Mildred's, but the one mile distance seemed shorter when she was able to meet with their neighbor's girl who was also in the sixth grade. Evan was pleased with his sister's progress. They talked together a lot about how it had been and about the future. At first, she had been apprehensive about his war wounds until he convinced her that they would not limit him at all once they were completely healed. Her greatest fear was to be left alone again. She continued to worry until she saw, with her own eyes, that her brother was getting stronger with each passing day.

Evan spent a lot of time considering his future. He thought of continuing school, but was uncertain what he wanted to do with his life. Nothing seemed important to him, and his indecision made him restless. The responsibility of caring for Amie had helped to motivate him. Her welfare became top priority in his plans for the future. That first night they spent in the old house he had sat at the kitchen table, which always seemed to be the center of activity in the home, and talked with her.

"This old house holds many happy memories for both of us, Amie. Just remember that Ma and Pa are always with us, sharing our lives from another world in which each of us return to. It's all right to miss them and to be saddened by their departure, but we have to look forward and try to live our lives as they would expect us to do."

She understood what he was trying to tell her. "I remember how sick they were with the fever. They suffered terribly, Evan. I could not ask God to continue their suffering for me. They both told me to be brave and strong. I tried, but it was hard…" she began to cry again.

Evan went around the table and embraced his sister. Only time could heal the pain of loss, all he could do was be there for her when she needed comfort and reinforcement.

He was feeling guilty not being with Roberta. He had waved and hollered to her and Bob as he passed by their place a few times, but did not stop. He had to straighten out his financial situation and get that responsibility off his shoulders. The day he went to Guilford to pick up the insurance check, he tried out a 1916 Studebaker coupe with very few miles for three hundred eighty dollars. He felt the need for greater mobility and an automobile would fulfill that function. He had learned to drive several types of vehicles in the Army. He gave a deposit on the vehicle and returned to Monson.

That same day, he and Amie walked to their parents' graves at the hillside cemetery south of the village. It turned out to be a tearful visit that helped to bring some closure to the burden of grief the two of them were carrying. The grave markers were made of gray Monson slate. The visit had been a catharsis for each of them. They left the site weakened and drained, but filled with a renewed sense of purpose.

Amie went to bed earlier than usual that evening. Evan sat at the table reviewing some of the important papers his parents had collected in a small wooden trunk. He had just finished reading the deed to the home and twenty-five acres of woodland when a knock came at the door.

"Come in," he called, turning to see who it was.

"It's me, Evan," Roberta replied in her soft melodious voice. "I saw you pass through town earlier today, and I've been wondering how you've been getting along." He rose to embrace her. She came into his arms. "I've expected to see you long before this. Is anything wrong?"

The familiar smell of bayberry in her hair brought back warm memories. "I simply had to get used to being here without Ma and Pa. I meant to stop by to see you and Bob... To be honest, I'm having a hard time adjusting to the responsibility, but I'm improving. It's nice to see you again. It really is."

His eyes were still a little red from the visit to the grave. They were brighter than the first time she saw him after he came home, even though they continued to reflect the trauma of combat and his return to an empty home. She kissed each eye.

"How is Amie doing?"

He released her and motioned her to a chair at the table. "She's doing better than I expected. I've already seen an improvement in her attitude since I showed up. It'll take time. I've been thinking a lot about the future. You and I had planned a lot of things, Roberta. Those memories were important to me, but now, things are not so simple."

The words stung her, and she replied with alarm, "What do you mean 'not so simple', Evan? I've loved you since we were small children. Those things we planned together are just as meaningful to me now as they were when we discussed them. Are you trying to tell me that you no longer want the same thing?"

"No. No…it's nothing like that, Roberta," he exclaimed, reaching for her hands across the table. "Perhaps now more than ever, I need your love and support, Roberta. I'm not as strong as I thought I would be, and with the added responsibility of Amie, I feel overwhelmed. I desperately want to make up for her loss. At times I think I might have gotten out of the hospital too quickly. Does that make any sense?"

"More than you know, gentle Evan. We'll just be patient and let time work its healing powers."

He smiled at her. "I've got a surprise. I'm going to purchase an automobile."

"That sounds like a wonderful first step towards the future. Bob told me that there are several openings at the quarry if you're interested."

He nodded his head. "I'm definitely not going to work in the quarries. I would much prefer working in the woods cutting logs and pulpwood. My first priority is to put up several cords of fuelwood ahead. By the way, it was generous of Bob to start us off with a load of dry wood, thanks. Sometime soon I'm also going to put in a bathroom now that the house has been wired for electricity. I could put it in the large closet downstairs."

"Wow, you've been doing a lot of thinking," she cried happily. "I've been asked to sing in an orchestra that a distant cousin is organizing in Dexter. We've already had a few practice sessions. They hope to play for local dances and other affairs. I'm thrilled. I can sing and get paid for it. I can't believe my good fortune."

"That's great. I'm glad for you. I haven't even looked at my old violin since I came home. I hope I haven't forgotten some of the old songs we liked to play."

"Don't fill your days with too much activity, Evan. You always seemed happiest when you were playing the violin. That last time I sang and you played our old favorite, *Danny Boy*, was a memorable performance that folks in town are still talking about. Find time for your music, Evan. Let it be a part of your healing process. Bob is still troubled by the things he experienced in France. Nightmares of the horrors wake him in the middle of the night sometimes. I feel so helpless trying to comfort him."

Evan shook his head in agreement, and soberly replied: "Time is the greatest healer, Roberta. What we saw and felt is unimaginable to the folks back home, and probably it's best that it remains that way. I'm handling it. Bob will deal with it, be patient with him. You've helped me more than you know. It's going to take a while for Bob and me to get back to normal. We'll always carry what we experienced in the war. Like it or not, it has become a part of our consciousness. Only the future will determine if we can overcome its influence."

She listened to what he was saying and saw that faraway look she had seen on Bob's face. It frightened her. She swept Evan in her arms and held him. "I'll always be there for you, dear Evan. Reach out for me, and I'll be there. Whatever you do, don't push me aside. I have loved you for so long and want to be a part of building your future... our future... Do you still want that?"

"Oh, my dearest Roberta. I can't imagine life without you." They kissed and held each other for a long time, drawing strength from their love. It was a defining moment each would look back on as a benchmark to measure their progress.

Before Roberta left, she told Evan that the ensemble she had signed on with was going to perform at the school reunion dance in the Tarr Hall at the foot of Tenney Hill. He promised to attend. It would be a fun evening renewing old friendships and acquaintances.

That night he checked on Amie, who was sleeping soundly, and reviewed his progress since he had arrived at home. He was satisfied with what he was accomplishing. Roberta left a warm glow in his heart. The thought that the two of them could plan a future together was gratifying; yet, there was a gnawing sense of deception. He had spent countless hours trying to figure out why Joleen would pay him the amount she offered to pose as her husband and father of the little boy, Alex. He almost confided the interlude to Roberta that evening, and declined at the last moment. He felt guilty keeping such a strange secret from her, but he had given his word and accepted the money. That committed him to living up to his promise even if it made him uncomfortable.

The next day, he drove Amie to school and stopped to pick up the mail at the Post Office. There was a letter from an attorney's office in Baltimore, Maryland, addressed to him. Sitting in the carriage while the mare headed back to the barn without any direction from him, he opened and read the letter:

Warren H. Hatch

Attorney-at-Law

Baltimore, Maryland

December 5, 1918

Dear Mr. Evan Mundy:

My law firm has been charged with settling the estate of Mister Lamont Carpenter, who died December 1, 1918. It is our intention to carry out his specific wishes to the best of our abilities.

You have been listed in his will as the beneficiary to receive the German violin manufactured by Gottlieb. The request was a recent addition to his will. The instrument will be sent to you as soon as we receive your signed and notarized signature on the enclosed document stating that you are the one and same person identified in the will. The document should be self-explanatory. If you have any questions, please contact us.

Thank you for your prompt attention to this matter.

Sincerely,
Warren Harry Hatch

Chapter Six

Several days after he signed the lawyer's document he received a package in the mail. Evan gently removed the fine instrument from the case and plucked the strings. It was still in tune from the last time he had used it. Placing it on his shoulder, he played several medleys of currently popular songs. The ancient violin had a deep and full sound that resonated with clarity, especially with the high notes. It had been a long time since Evan had played a violin, except that brief moment for Lamont Carpenter; yet, even his untrained ear could detect the difference the expensive instrument made. Notes had a softer and fuller expression, giving the notes a "feel" and a tone his own instrument could not duplicate.

While he was admiring the instrument, Bob Gibson appeared at the front door of the house. Evan quickly put the violin back in its case and opened the door for his friend.

"Come in, Bob. You don't have to knock."

"I was enjoying the music and didn't want to intrude," Bob told him. "You've still got a nice soft touch on the fiddle, Evan. You should play more."

Bob Gibson and Roberta were twins, but they did not look alike. As a matter of fact, they were opposites in demeanor and were quite competitive with each other. Bob's blond hair and blue eyes reflected his Finnish ancestry. He was a hard-working young man who had a tendency to be somewhat more reclusive than his sister. He usually spoke only when he was directly addressed. Ever since he was a small boy he had selected his friends carefully. Evan was his closest friend. He was severely gassed in France, with burns over a large portion of his body from the deadly mustard gas used by the Germans. The gas affected his lungs, limiting severe activity, but Bob passed it off as insignificant. He was glad to be alive and back at home where he had yearned to be.

"How about a cup of coffee, Bob?"

"If you're brewing some, I'll join you, Evan. It's really nice to have you back home. I was thinking it would be great to go hunting together again like we used to. Deer season is still on."

Evan led him into the kitchen where he threw a couple of small pieces of firewood into the kitchen stove and opened the damper in the flue. By the time he placed the coffee pot over the front covers of the stove, it was roaring to life.

"I have an apple pie from Aunt Mildred that would go good with a coffee. What do you say?" Evan casually asked, knowing that Bob had a voracious appetite for anything sweet.

"You know me," he laughed out loud. "I never refuse dessert. Your aunt makes the best pies in town. This is like old times, sitting in this kitchen where I've spent many happy hours with you and your folks. It's kind of hard. I thought the war was bad enough, but returning home to see all of the deaths here in such a short time was difficult to handle. How are you doing really, Ev?" Evan knew that his friend was one to hold his grief inside out of view. It was visible in his sad eyes.

"It has been hard, Bob. I think Amie helped a lot. Being responsible for her the way Ma and Pa would want made it easier. How about Roberta? She was so close to your mother. It must have been rough on her."

"Oh my," Bob replied. "You would not believe how she carried on. I was concerned for her sanity, really. She withdrew for days without saying a thing or eating a mouthful. She kept repeating that Mom had promised to knit a new shawl for her and that it was not fair that she could not keep that promise."

"She seems to be handling things better now," Evan added.

"I think her concern for your welfare helped her some, Evan. She loves you a lot. She started to be more like her old self that first day you came home." Bob watched Evan cut the apple pie and asked, "Would I be prying too much if I asked you when the two of you are going to tie the knot?"

Evan smiled, pouring the coffee. "Bob, you ask too many questions. Your sister and I have not discussed it since I came home. My responsibility to Amie has to be considered, and this new singing position she's so happy and excited about hasn't left much room for either of us to consider our future. I'm really pleased for her to have a chance to sing professionally. I think we all hoped and thought that it would happen someday. She has a wonderful voice that should be shared by a larger audience than this small town in central Maine."

Bob understood what his friend was telling him. "Well, your time will come when its right for you both."

Evan changed the subject. "How are things at the quarry? Roberta suggested that I take a job there. It's kind of hard to explain, but I just don't want that kind of a job. Maybe I want too much. To be honest, I've felt sort of lost and don't know where to go from here. Returning home to pick up the threads of my life where I left them two years ago has been a disappointing experience. Something besides the loss of parents is missing, and I can't explain what it is."

"Ah, my friend, I'm relieved to hear you say that. I've been feeling the same way. The death of Mom and Dad was a reality that had to be faced squarely soon after my discharge from the Army. There was no money, and bills had to be paid, so I took the quarry job because it was available. I really wanted to go on to school and learn a trade, but life goes on... I'm not unhappy about events, just a little disappointed. Maybe Roberta will be able to establish herself in the music world. I hope so. Does that complicate your relationship, Evan?"

He thought about the question and replied, "No, I'm as happy for her as you. Our time will come. This is probably a good time for her to step out in the world beyond Monson and grasp the opportunities that are out there. She'll never be satisfied until she explores that world on her own terms. I hope she'll find fulfillment."

"I hope so, too," Bob exclaimed. "By the way, I spoke to Jake Collins, the game warden for this area, and he told me that there was an opening for an assistant warden. I thought of you when he mentioned it."

"That kind of a job could be interesting. Did Jake elaborate on the rate of pay or anything else?"

"Not to me, Evan. He was in a hurry as usual. I noticed that the state has supplied him with a Ford automobile. Well,"

Bob announced, finishing his cup of coffee, "I've got to get the cows in for milking. It's great to have you back home, Evan."

Two days after Bob's visit, Evan picked up his new automobile and made an appointment with Jake Collins, intending to apply for the job with the State of Maine. Jake Collins, who lived on the Greenville Road, had been a good friend of his father. He had the reputation of being fair and reasonable to the legions of hunters and fishermen in the area around Monson north to Moosehead Lake. Evan's Uncle Del frequently acted as a guide and outfitter for hunting and fishing parties into the inaccessible regions of the vast northern woods. He had a strong, long-lasting friendship with Jake and always praised him for his good common sense.

Collins met Evan at the door of his home and invited him into his warm kitchen. "Come in, Evan. It's nice to see that you've recovered from your wounds. You had all of us worried for a while. Sorry about your ma and pa. Your pa was a close friend that a person could depend on to do the right thing. I'd like to think that you're cut from the same cloth. We're proud of your service record. Please sit at the table. I've got a fresh pot of coffee on the stove and some fresh boulla rolls from my lovely Finnish daughter-in-law."

"I'd enjoy a coffee and a boulla roll, Mr. Collins. I guess everyone in Monson is addicted to them by now. Since I came home, I've been a little restless and unsure of what I want to do. Bob Gibson told me about the available assistant warden job the other day. I've been thinking about it and was wondering what's involved. As you well know, pa and I were enthusiastic hunters and fishermen. If I had a choice, I'd prefer to work out-of-doors than in a dusty quarry job sanding chalk boards."

Jake observed this young soldier whom he had watched grow into manhood. There was a quiet confidence about him that made a person feel at ease in his presence. Jake knew that quality came from his father. "The opening available has generated quite a bit of interest. If you are interested, I'll be glad to recommend you for the position, Evan. The job comes with some risk. There's a small percentage of people who do not accept authority and resist when confronted. The Maine Game Warden Service began forty years ago, and several wardens have been shot to death while carrying out their duties."

"I never had any trouble maintaining discipline in my company, Sir," Evan firmly replied.

"I'm sure you didn't, Son. The position will require you to be away from home on occasion. I know that you have your younger sister to care for."

"I've thought about that possibility and talked to Amie. She can stay with my Uncle Del and Aunt Mildred any time it's necessary."

Jake Collins was a legend in the great Maine woods. His formidable size and booming voice helped him do his job with fairness and common sense. His intimidating presence belied the very kind and caring man that was his nature. The true sportsmen saw him as a friend. Those who violated the Maine conservation laws found him to be a tenacious defender of the rule of law. He had been wounded and attacked countless times during the performance of his duties. His dedication to those who were lost in the wilderness generated a ray of hope to those unfortunate people. The Maine Game Warden Service had an enviable record of performance in the search and rescue phases of their responsibilities to the state. Jake Collins probably headed more relief missions in the forest than any other man in the service.

Evan was told that the job would be his if he passed the rigid physical and maintained an acceptable level of achievement in the required training period at Augusta. The school was similar to the one required for the Maine State Police, with an emphasis on conservation related laws and policies. The job paid two dollars per day plus expenses. He filled out an application for the position with Jake Collins and left his house with a glow of satisfaction.

On his way home, he stopped at the Gibson farmhouse to share his good fortune. "I think I've found something that fits me, Bob," he exclaimed excitedly, describing his conversation with Collins.

"I'm glad for you, Evan. Roberta and I were just talking about you and Amie. She told me that she was going up on Lookout Rock to watch the sun go down over Russell Mountain," Bob said.

The spectacular view from the hill south of his house on their woodlands had been a favorite spot for both of them over the years. He had not taken time to visit the familiar location since his homecoming. The fact that Roberta retreated to the site brought back a lot of warm memories that were an important part of their youth.

"I haven't been up there yet. I think I'll join her. I'll see you later, Bob."

Evan drove his automobile to his house and walked across the roadway to the well-worn woods road that led straight up the hill. A trail branched off the skid road to a series of rock outcrops with a few large white pine trees growing out of breaks in the granite fissures, spreading their erratic limbs over the mesa-like formations. They had found it when they were in the first grade.

From the elevated platform they could see the lake and their two houses on the roadway below. Russell Mountain rose above a relatively low-lying terrain highlighting its massive dome-shaped peak. The evening sun always settled behind the promontory in the wintertime. It was a place of great beauty when the sinking rays reflected off the water, giving it a silvery sheen just before they slowly disappeared behind the mountain.

Just as Evan reached the top he heard Roberta crying. She was sitting with her back resting against one of the massive white pine trees, looking out across the lake. Not wanting to intrude upon her moment of solitude, he paused a few moments before announcing himself.

"Roberta, it's me, Evan. Bob told me you came up here."

She had seen him park his new automobile in the driveway and cross the road. "I've been expecting you. I'm okay. I've been thinking a lot lately. Ever since the terrible flu epidemic, everything seems to be so difficult."

Evan took a seat close beside her against the same tree and reached out for her hand. "I'm a little out of breath. The climb is steeper than I remembered. Tell me, why are you crying?"

She squeezed his hand. "I know that everyone who experienced losses has the same kind of sorrow and yearning for the way things used to be. I was so glad and relieved to have you home, Evan. Yet, even that was not the same. I know that I'm probably being selfish, but you came home a stranger…"

In the past they had frequently sat at the lookout rock for long periods of time without talking. It was enough to simply be together, humbled by the view before them. The setting sun added a whole new dimension to the scene, painting the horizon and the water below with vibrant splashes of red and orange hues that completely enveloped the western skies.

"I'm sorry if I've failed to measure up for you, Roberta."

"I understand that you and Bob have been through a lot in the war. Maybe I was immature to think that we could pick up our lives where we left off before you shipped out to France. It hasn't been the same. You've been distant and preoccupied with Amie, which I understand, but whether you agree or not, you've treated our relationship with some indifference, and I don't know why. Is there someone else in your life?"

The scathing question brought back memories of the Joleen Carpenter incident. He agonized that he could not explain what took place. Roberta's intuitive nature had picked up on his dilemma! How should he handle the delicate situation he was honor bound to keep to himself?

He placed an arm around her and pulled her close. "No, Roberta, there's no one else in my life. How can I explain how much your love has meant to me when I was alone and frightened on the battlefield? The fact that you have perceived Bob and me as different people is true. My God, how can a person experience such bloodshed and not be changed forever by its ugliness? Please, do not doubt the sincerity and depth of my love for you. Dry those tears and give me a little more time to adjust to home life. Much has changed for both of us. Our love for each other should be strong enough to overcome any obstacles."

"It is, Evan. It is, and I'm sorry if I've doubted your commitment to our future. The flu has left all of us traumatized and bewildered. I'm sure it has complicated your adjustment even more than the rest of us."

He kissed her on the temple. "No more tears, Roberta. I came up here to share some good news with you. I just spoke to Bob about it."

She turned to look into his eyes. "Tell me that you still love me."

"If you could look in my heart, you'd know how much I love you. I'm happy that our future is beginning to look a little brighter. I've just been offered a job as Jake Collins' assistant game warden, and I accepted. I've been worried about the prospects of a job. The quarries are out for me. I'd rather cut pulpwood than work in the slate quarry."

"Jake Collins' assistant!" she cried. "That's great, Evan. You'll be a good officer. I'm so proud of you. Now, I've got some news to share with you, too. As I've already mentioned, I've been offered a job as singer in an orchestra. The leader just informed me that he has a three month contract for January, February and March to perform at a club in Boston. What do you think about that?"

"It sounds like a great opportunity for you, Roberta. You have the kind of voice that should be enjoyed by larger audiences than you could reach here in Maine. Of course, I'll miss you while you're gone. It's a chance of a lifetime, and you should embrace it."

She kissed him softly on the lips. "To be really honest, Evan. I've been tormented by the chance because it means I'll be away from you and Bob at this crucial time in your adjustment to the domestic life in a town that has been altered almost as badly as if we had been in a war. I've felt as if I was abandoning both you and Amie for selfish reasons. Thank you for being so understanding. How lucky I am to have won your affection."

They spent an hour sitting together at the lookout remembering how it had been when they were small children. Roberta begged Evan to dust off his old violin so that he could play at the annual alumni social at Tarr's Hall on Tenney Hill. He agreed provided she did their trademark tradition of *DANNY BOY*. The event sounded like fun.

The only down side to the event was the guilt he harbored about the Gottlieb violin from Joleen's father. How could he ever explain owning such a priceless instrument and maintain his solemn pledge of silence to Joleen? He answered the question by placing the violin on the closet shelf out of sight and out of mind. At some time in the future, a way would be found...

46

Chapter Seven

Two weeks later, Evan was ready for the Alumni dance. He had practiced every night on his old violin after replacing all of the strings. The valuable Gottlieb was temporarily placed underneath several boxes in the attic. He was able to dismiss the incident for the time being. Bob and Evan went to the dance in their best regulation Army uniforms. Actually, he was still officially in the Army. His discharge papers had not arrived.

Amie was excited about the affair. Her brother had promised that she could attend wearing her best dress, a dark blue one trimmed in white lace. Earlier that afternoon before the dance, Roberta had come to trim her long hair and combed the braids out so that it hung full about her shoulders.

Evan entered the house after feeding and watering the two horses in the barn. "My, my. I'm going to accompany two of the loveliest ladies in town to the alumni dance. You look very nice, Amie."

"Will you dance with me, Evan?" she asked, looking up at him with a big grin.

"Sure, if you promise to not complain about my dancing," he teased.

"He does better than he thinks, Amie," Roberta added, noticing that the deep lines around his eyes were less pronounced since their time alone on Lookout Rock. "I've got to go home to get ready. I'll see the two of you at the hall."

"You can ride with us if you want," Evan offered, a little disappointed.

"Thanks, but I've got to be at the hall a little early to go over some routines with the orchestra leader."

"I'm kind of nervous about playing accompaniment with a full orchestra," he admitted.

"Oh, no, Evan. I told them that you alone would accompany me for a couple of songs. You know how it is, the first hour will probably be taken up with speeches. You and I will have the segment immediately after that. Don't worry, you'll do just fine. I'm a bundle of nerves about tonight," she laughed.

"Tell Bob we'll pick him up in our new automobile."

"I will," she replied, kissing Evan on her way out the door.

The alumni gathering was one of the favorite social events of the year. Classmates turned out in large numbers to attend and reminisce with friends and neighbors. Most of the town was made up of Swedish and Finnish second-year immigrants who had come to work in the three slate quarries scattered all over the town. There was a strong patriotic fervor that bonded the family-oriented Scandinavian culture.

Amie walked from the automobile to the hall between Bob and her brother, holding their hands. Everyone they met congratulated Bob and Evan for their service and were thankful that they had returned home. Monson had lost five men in the war. The devastation of the war and the flu epidemic was responsible for the sober and nostalgic air that permeated feelings at the dance. Still, their coming together in fellowship and community was a manifestation of their love of country.

There was one very special and beloved teacher at the Monson Academy High School, Miss Weymouth. She taught math and science for several years, spanning two generations of students. She never married, but her family included all the students who had passed through her classroom for the past thirty years. She wore her white hair wrapped in a bun fastened at the back of her head. With her soft voice and big heart she quickly won everyone's affection and inspired maximum effort from her students without asking for it directly. Beneath the veneer of fragility was a strong demanding woman who vented her displeasure every once in a while in the classroom. Those who experienced it or were the object of her concern never forgot the outburst.

Traditionally, Miss Weymouth's talk was the high spot of the alumni affair, and she enjoyed being the center of attention among her "children". She retained a slight southern drawl and pronounced every word distinctly. No one ever misunderstood her. She wore glasses that always crept down to the tip of her nose, hanging precariously. She frequently pushed them back to the bridge of her nose, thus starting the cycle all over again. Some students, including Evan, used to count the times she did it during the class of one hour each. His best count was thirty-four against Roberta's thirty-seven.

Miss Weymouth was introduced by the Principal, Mr. Holden, holding out his arm for her to come up onto the stage. She smiled at him and turned to the waiting audience: "Dear friends, students and fellow Monsonites, how pleased I am to once again address you all at this traditional gathering of alumni. We have recently witnessed the tragedy of the flu epidemic that has circled the world in search of victims. It came on the heels of a war that has cost our small community much grief and sadness. Monson men were quick to answer the call to arms. How proud we are of your gallant service on our behalf. To those of you who have returned to our bosom we sigh, 'thank God.' Some of you will carry the emotional scars of combat with you the rest of your lives. It is our prayers that the peace and harmony that you seek will be found here in the hearts of those who nurtured you and saw you grow from infant to manhood. We don't have time to single out everyone who served. However, before I close, I'd like to mention two men who have received wounds in combat and returned home to find that both parents were victims of the flu. I know you're out there, Evan Mundy and Robert Gibson. Please raise your hands."

The hall erupted in a thunderous demonstration of pent up energy. Shouts of "welcome home" mingled with clapping and stomping of feet for a long time. Evan was never comfortable in a crowd, but these were his people, and he and Bob appreciated their display of support. After Miss Weymouth's speech, they finished the meal prepared by local cooks and looked forward to the musical portion of the annual event.

Roberta had told Evan that there was a slight change in their schedule. The orchestra would open up first with a couple of sets prior to their solo segment. The small stage began to fill up with musicians. The orchestra leader, Victor Turin, was a tall young Italian with dark complexion and coal black hair. He played the trombone and stepped to the center of the stage, raising his hands for their attention.

"Ladies and gentlemen, it is our pleasure to provide music for the annual alumni social here in Monson. Our unit is composed of two violins, my trombone, a base fiddle, two clarinets and piano. Collectively we call ourselves the Turin Players. We are especially pleased to announce that our vocalist is one of your very own. Tonight is her first appearance with the orchestra. Let's give her a warm welcome, Miss Roberta Gibson."

Roberta walked to the center of the stage. She was beautiful in a teal gown with white lace covering her throat. Evan had never seen her more lovely. She scanned the audience to locate him and waved. "Thank you… thank you, dear friends and neighbors. It has been a privilege to sing for you at several town affairs, and your enthusiasm has been encouraging. Tonight we're going to start the evening off with a few old favorites. I hope you enjoy them."

The orchestra sounded a loud crescendo and immediately began a medley of popular songs. For the next three quarters of an hour Roberta sang *Carolina in the Morning; Keep the Home Fires Burning; There's A Long, Long Trail; Roses of Picady; and Till We Meet Again.*

She took a break after each song while the orchestra played some popular dance numbers. She asked Evan to dance the first waltz with her.

"You're lovely tonight, Roberta," he told her. "I think your voice has improved since I last heard you sing. The musicians are really good. The violinists are above average, that's for sure. Are you certain you want me to accompany you tonight?"

"Hush now, Evan. Of course I want that. I want the people, our people, to experience the unique touch you bring to the instrument. That last time we performed, before you left for the war, the town talked about it for a long time. I'd like to capture that same mood again if we can. I love you, Evan Mundy, and I will be proud to someday be your wife. You look handsome in your uniform. In case you haven't noticed, the girls have been eyeing you all evening."

He blushed again. "How nice it is to be home with friends. Visiting with a lot of the old school gang has made my day. I'm glad you prodded me to come. Bob seems to be enjoying himself with Joyce Hammer. The way they look at each other leads me to believe that something special is taking place. I remember her in school. She's a good person and will be good for Bob."

"I've known about their attraction for each other for a while. He needs someone in his life. Are you nervous about playing tonight?"

"To be honest, yes. We're among friends that will excuse a mistake if I goof. Actually, I'm looking forward to it just the same. You have a beautiful voice that warrants a full orchestra backing you up. I'm very proud of you. I have no doubt that your voice will be appreciated wherever you perform."

"Your support is important to me, Evan. I'd never dare to venture so far away from home if you did not approve." She held him close and placed her head against his shoulder. "Thank you for being so understanding. I'm glad you're taking the job with Jake Collins. I'll worry about you though. The job is not without risk. I've read that several game wardens have been shot while performing their duties."

"Compared to the way it was in France, the warden job will be a piece of cake. I've always loved the forest, and this job gives me a chance to earn a living in that environment. Who could ask for anything more? My only concern is for Amie."

"What do you mean, Evan?"

"Well, I could be away at night occasionally on patrols or investigations far from home conducting search and rescue operations. Jake told me he spends almost half of his time on searching for lost persons. I've spoken to Amie about it, and she is perfectly willing to stay with Aunt Mildred. Bob even volunteered sometimes."

"When I'm home I'd be glad to stay with her at your house," she replied, watching the band wind down on their set of slow waltzes.

Evan escorted her to the stage steps and waved at Victor Turin. He returned to the table where Bob and Joyce were sitting. She was an attractive girl with long blonde hair and blue eyes, reflecting her Finnish mother. She had been a classmate in school with Bob and Evan. Everyone liked her calm and modest demeanor. Upon approaching the small table, he noted the way they looked at each other. He had never seen his best friend so happy.

"You two looked good out there," he exclaimed. "It's nice to see you again, Joyce. It seems a long time since we were in Miss Weymouth's physics class."

"You and Bob look good in your uniforms. I was relieved when the two of you returned home where we know you are safe." She looked questioningly at Bob. "Do you want to tell him the news?"

Bob patted her on the arm and turned to Evan. "You're the first to know that Joyce and I are engaged. We're planning a wedding come next June. Will you be my best man?"

It was not unexpected. "I'll be honored to be your best man. You're already my best friend. I'm happy for the two of you. You're getting the best, Joyce. My, what a surprise, congratulations." He bent over and kissed her on the cheek. "My friend has made a wise choice. I hope you'll be happy."

"My sister is beaming over the chance to sing with the orchestra. She was reluctant to commit herself to so much time away from home. It looks as if the two of you are poised on the threshold of new adventures in your lives. I hope it brings you contentment. You and Roberta are a natural together. I hope someday to call my best friend my brother-in-law."

Evan blushed. "I'm hopeful that may be a reality sometime in the future. Right now, both of us have to play the cards we've been handed."

Later in the evening, the orchestra ended their final dance set and began to vacate the stage. Victor Turin thanked the people and turned the stage over to Miss Weymouth. She climbed the steps to the stage telling the audience that the best was saved for the last. Monson's very own Roberta Gibson and Evan Mundy were going to perform a tradition that had been popular prior to the war. "Sit back and relax and enjoy the experience. Thank you all and God Bless."

He was so proud of Roberta. She held out her hands for the crowd to be quiet and announced, "I'm sure that some of you will recall that alumni social several years ago when Evan and I did a few songs before he left for the Army along with my brother and others in town. It turned out to be a wonderful memory that sustained many of us through the war years. We are going to duplicate the same program tonight. The first is an old folk song favorite, *Lorena*."

She turned to smile at Evan, who played a short introduction to the popular ballad. He was always nervous in front of a group of people. Tonight, he was anxious, but as soon as he lifted the violin to his shoulder, his jitters disappeared and a calm confidence enveloped him. Music always had that magic touch.

The hall was silent. Not a word or a movement could be heard as the townspeople listened to the soft vibrant tones from his violin. Using long sweeps of the bow, he set the mood for the melancholic folk song that had never lost its ability to tug at the heartstrings. Older folks recalled their romantic moments of youth and the young hoped for such a love as the lovely Lorena portrayed.

Roberta stood on the small stage and filled the hall with her clear soprano voice, holding out her hands beseeching the audience to share the hope, the joy and the sadness of love. Her voice carried to every part of the hall, holding the audience in the palm of her hands. It was a memorable performance. Evan was so proud of her.

They performed *Blue Moon*, *The Last Rose of Summer*, and the all-time favorite of the performers and the audience, *Danny Boy*. Whenever he played the popular Irish folk song, he became immersed in the sadness of the story. The lyrics had their moments of high emotional involvement. When it ended, it always left him feeling that he did not want it to end. His playing telegraphed the emotion, and the audience knew that, once again, they were experiencing something special.

Roberta completed the song with moist eyes. It always did that to her. She turned to Evan and saw that he, too, was caught up in the same emotion. She embraced him. "You were wonderful, Evan. I'm so proud of you."

That evening became a part of their collective registry of memories they would never forget. It had bound them with a vow of devotion and a promise that their tomorrows would be shared together.

Chapter Eight

Two Years Later, December, 1920.

Evan hunkered down in the balsam fir thicket waiting for the sun to go down. The night was clear and cold. He fingered the small thermos bottle filled with hot coffee and poured a small serving in the cup. It tasted good. He smiled, recalling how Amie had insisted that she send him off with something hot. This could be a long uneventful evening and he planned to ration the warming brew.

The thicket was at the edge of an abandoned apple orchard which was an attraction for the deer population in the area. It was isolated, yet accessible by an abandoned road when the county restructured the main road from Shirley to Greenville. Poaching had been a problem. Evan was outraged when he found several deer carcasses left to rot. They had been shot by poachers who took only the trophy-size antlers, leaving the animals to rot in the forest. The despicable acts were a threat to the true sportsmen and an affront to the citizens of the state who view their wildlife population as a precious resource to be managed with care.

Much had changed in the past two years. Jake Collins had died from wounds received when he tried to arrest two well-armed poachers. He was a much respected man with a love for the Maine wilderness. Evan had come to love the gentle man with the booming voice who treated him as an equal. He had looked upon Jake as a mentor. Once Evan appeared in August for orientation and training to be a game warden, he was content that he had found his life work in the great outdoors he had always loved. He enjoyed carrying out wildlife population surveys, making a point early in his indoctrination to the service to document everything he observed during his forest travels in his private journal. The ledger became a

54

passion for him. It answered the basic questions of what, when, and where, especially for habitat information. He was uniquely qualified as a spokesman for the public relations aspect of his job. Public trust and support was the main ingredient in any successful wildlife regulatory agency.

The only drawback to the successful conduct of his position was that it took him away from home a lot. Thankfully, Amie was able to stay with Aunt Mildred and, at times, she stayed with Bob and his new bride, Joyce. Amie and Evan made the most of the time they had together. She frequently accompanied him whenever he had to appear in court after an arrest. When he was not in the field on regular patrols, he spoke to granges, high school students, and church groups, often bringing her along. She enjoyed seeing her big brother being the center of attention.

Evan sat in the thicket waiting to determine if any poachers would show up that evening. Sitting alone in the cold night air, his thoughts often turned to Roberta. Her singing career was going better than anticipated. She had already made a recording with the Victor Turin orchestra for the RCA Victrola Company. The songs were *My Blue Heaven* and *Last Rose of Summer*. They became very popular, and the orchestra was more in demand than ever.

Over the past two years, Roberta and Evan saw each other only at Christmas, Thanksgiving, and Fourth of July, and then only for a few days. They maintained a steady flow of letters to each other. He was lonely at times, but he never complained. Neither of them were happy with the prolonged absences from home. Roberta had confided in him that if she could obtain a contract to do records, then she would gladly give up the exhausting daily engagements in different towns for weeks on end. She was finding the routine burdensome. Most of all, she was concerned that the choice of songs was less and less hers to make. Young producers and talent handlers arrogantly thought they had a special insight into what the public wanted to hear.

At about midnight, Evan was alerted by lights coming down the road before he heard the engine of a large sedan pull into the line of apple trees. He had hidden his State of Maine Ford in an abandoned gravel pit deeper in the woods beyond the orchard where it could not be seen by a vehicle entering the orchard.

Hopefully, no one was aware that he was in a good position to cut off their exit from the orchard. His first problem was to determine how many men were involved. The headlights shone down a row of trees picking up several pairs of eyes from curious deer staring into the glare. One was a stately buck with at least a ten point set of antlers, a worthwhile trophy. He heard a man's voice calmly ask someone to get out the 30-30 rifle. That meant that he had to deal with at least two armed men!

Unwilling to wait until they shot the animal, Evan quietly left his isolated location, circling around to the rear of the vehicle, blocking the road they used to enter the orchard. From that vantage point he could see the outline of three men from the glare of the headlights. Two men were leaning against the front fenders to steady their aim into the curious herd. A third man stood on the right side.

Evan carefully removed his service .38 caliber revolver with his right hand while holding a powerful three-battery flashlight away from his body in his left hand. He was close enough that he could accurately fire the revolver, if necessary, and still accomplish an arrest on his terms. All three men were visible to him. He turned the flashlight directly on the man leaning against the right fender.

"Drop your weapons or the first to be shot will be the man in the light. Do it now!"

The shooter in the glare of the light was the first to throw his rifle on the ground. The one standing beside him followed suit. The shooter on the left fender had dropped to the ground out of sight, creating a dangerous situation for Evan. He raised his voice warning, "Don't try anything. There's no need of bloodshed for the sake of a trophy antler. You on the driver's side of the vehicle, stand and raise your hands. I promise to shoot the man in the light even if you shoot me..."

"God damn it, John. He's got me blinded, stand up and show yourself," screamed the man in the light.

With that outburst, the three men came together in the glare of the light. "That's fine. Now, lay down on the ground with your heads facing toward the deer herd and place your hands in the small of your back. Hurry now, this Colt revolver has a hair trigger, and my finger is getting cold."

The three men were quick to comply. Relieved that the situation had been handled better than anticipated, Evan placed wrist bracelets on each of the men. Just as he finished securing the third man, he turned to look into the automobile. The rear door was partially open. Flame from a rifle barrel aimed at him exploded, hitting him on the left hip, spinning him around, dropping the flashlight. His instincts served Evan well. He fired two shots from his revolver at the dark void around the flaming barrel. A hot burning sensation stung his midsection. He desperately held on to the revolver and reached to retrieve the flashlight on the ground beside him.

Shining the light into the open door, he saw a man sprawled halfway across the doorsill. Thinking that he might be faking, Evan carefully stood up and examined the man. He was dead, shot twice in the chest!

The three men were still lying on the ground. Evan knew he had to act quickly. Even if the wound he had was not serious, it could disable him, creating a dangerous situation. Ordering the three men to stand and back into a circle so that he could bind them together with a stout piece of rawhide he always carried with him, he again checked the man in the car, detecting no pulse.

"You three men are responsible for this tragedy tonight. None of you warned me of the presence of the fourth man. Now walk in front of me where the light is shining. Move!"

He loaded the men into his Ford and drove to his regional headquarters at Greenville, feeling weaker by the minute. Greenville police took the men into custody while his fellow wardens whisked him to the emergency room of the Greenville Hospital. Blood had been draining from his wounds so that by the time he arrived at headquarters, he was too weak to get out of the vehicle on his own.

He was immediately hooked up to blood plasma. The physician noted that his pistol belt had deflected the rifle bullet away from his heart, probably saving his life. The physician cut away his clothing to explore the wound. The bullet had entered the bottom of his rib cage, breaking one or more of his ribs, exiting in the fleshy area near his hip. He was fortunate! Evan had remained unconscious through the time he was in the emergency room. The doctor cleansed the bullet punctures and dressed them with heavy gauze. The ribs would mend themselves in time, requiring no surgery.

The next morning, his body ached all over. The first thing he saw was Amie and Bob sitting beside the bed with worried looks on their faces. Amie saw him blink his eyes, and leaned down to whisper in his ear. "Can you hear me, Evan?"

"I hear you, Amie," he replied with a thick tongue. "How long have you been here?"

The dark lines around her eyes softened when she smiled. "Mister Gibson and I came just as soon as the warden told us that you had been hurt. We've been worried about you."

A nurse came into the room to take his pulse, temperature, and blood pressure. She asked if he was hungry or thirsty, suggesting that he should drink all he could hold to replace his lost blood. He asked for a cup of coffee and a piece of toast, which pleased the nurse and his two visitors. His passion for coffee was a good sign.

Bob and Amie chatted with him for a few minutes, promising to return the next day. Shortly after they left, his regional supervisor and a state policeman assigned to the district stopped to question him about the incident. The three men in custody and the one Evan killed were all from New York City. They had been staying at a hunting lodge for several days during the hunting season and had hopes of returning with more deer meat than they obtained legally.

Evan's district supervisor, Captain James Melee, was angry that Evan attempted to make an arrest without assistance. He could have been killed and left in the isolated area while the men departed out of the state. He was shot with a Winchester Model 94 .32 special caliber rifle, which could have blown away half of his chest if the cartridge had not been deflected. Evan was ordered to take off at least a week after the hospital discharged him. He had no objection to the order.

That first night in the hospital reminded him of other hospitals. They were all pretty much the same, with sounds, smells, and apprehensive atmospheres being universal. He had trouble sleeping. His close call did not worry him as much as the fact that he had taken the life of another man. All night he wondered how the man's family was going to react to their loss. Even though he was a stranger who had tried to kill him,

Evan felt bad for having been placed in that position. It was his first death as a warden, and he searched for what he had done wrong. Captain Melee was correct; he should have asked for help on the stakeout.

His first impulse, the next day, was to write to Roberta, explaining his stay in the hospital. He dismissed it. If he was strong enough he planned to go to Boston to tell her in person. When Amie and Bob arrived at the hospital, the attending doctor told him he could go home as long as he changed the dressing every day and rested. His rib cage would be sore for a week or so until the bones were mended. Moderate exercise was recommended, but aggressive workouts or erratic movements could be dangerous.

Amie had a week off from school until the second week in January and looked forward to caring for her big brother. He agreed to take her with him to Boston. It would be her first trip out of the state of Maine, and she was thrilled at the possibility. First, she insisted, her brother had to rest and recover his strength, or he could have a relapse. She had promised the doctor to take good care of him.

Two days after his release from the hospital, they left Monson on the Monson narrow gauge train for Brownville Junction where they made connections to Newport for the Boston and Maine train to Boston. They took a taxi to the Lennox Hotel on Boylston Street behind the Boston Public Library just off Copley Square, taking a room on the eighth floor with a view overlooking the New York Central rail yards. Amie was all eyes, impressed with the hustle and bustle of the city and the energy that permeated its busy streets.

Anxious to see Roberta, they took a cab to the Copley Hotel, an exclusive hotel for the elites and well-off visitors to the city. The elegant interior of the hotel lobby made Evan feel out of place and a little awkward. They inquired at the desk for Roberta Gibson's room. The clerk told them that she was not in and asked if he wanted to leave a message for her?

Disappointed, Evan declined to leave word. He wanted his presence to be a surprise. He was not as strong as he thought he would be, so he and Amie returned to their room so that he could rest. Amie watched the world around her from the hotel windows. Traffic and pedestrians filled the streets below. She wondered what everyone was doing and where they were going. It was in sharp contrast to Monson.

A few hours later, they had dinner at their hotel and then walked around the block to the Copley again. Instead of asking if she was in, Evan decided to take a chance and went directly to her room which he knew to be number 388. Tingling with excitement, they got off the elevator on the third floor and located her room.

"This will sure surprise her," he whispered to Amie, knocking on the door. No one answered, yet he heard muffled voices inside.

He knocked again, louder than before. A man's voice called out to wait a second. Evan was afraid he had the wrong room and double checked the number on one of the letters from Roberta with her return address. Finally, the door opened. Victor Turin looked down at Amie and then at Evan, not recognizing him. "What do you want?" he asked brusquely.

"I've come to see Roberta Gibson. Do I have the correct room?" Evan asked, pushing the door open wider. Amie stayed in the corridor. Unprepared for what he discovered, Evan swore, "My God, I can't believe..."

His sentence was lost by a loud scream from Roberta, sitting on the bed in an advance stage of nakedness. "No... no! What are you doing here?" she screamed incoherently.

Amie heard the scream and stepped through the door beside her brother, shocked at what she saw. Evan felt as if he had been struck a heavy blow. Speechless, he stared at Roberta sitting on the bed holding a sheet in front of herself. This was not his Roberta. This was a stranger who looked like her. Amie saw the turmoil exploding in his head and gently took him by the arm and led him out of the hotel room. Cries of disbelief and despair echoed from the room.

"Come, Evan, let's go home."

Chapter Nine

The train ride home from Boston was the longest, most difficult trip Evan had ever taken. Amie was constantly at his side. Several times large tears welled in his eyes and rolled down across his face, regardless of how much he tried to hide his pain from her. She encouraged him to let it out and not to hold it back. His silence and his despair frightened her.

The deception stung deeply. Surprisingly, not one word of condemnation came from his lips. Amie visualized that if it had been done to her, she would have taken great delight in calling her every vile name she could think of. His silence about the despicable betrayal was especially worrisome. He simply stared at the passing landscape from the train window.

He told Amie that he was going to join the Army National Guard in Greenville. He missed the camaraderie that existed in the military. Joining would give him extra money, which he could use, and help prepare him for the various duties that were a part of being a game warden in Maine. It was as if he felt a need to fill his days with more activity than had been his norm. Amie saw it as his way of handling the loss of Roberta.

The day after they arrived home, Evan went to visit with Bob, catching him in the shelter attached to the barn splitting wood. "You're home earlier than expected. How did you and Amie like Boston? Bob saw the strained demeanor and the dark circles under his eyes. "My God, what's wrong, Evan? Has something happened to Roberta?"

"I wanted to talk with you, Bob. Your sister is doing fine; you don't have to worry about her. I've got a request to make, and I never dreamed that I'd ask such a thing of my best friend."

"I've never seen you like this, Evan."

"Well, I've got to tell you that your sister and I are finished…"

"Finished... what do you mean?"

"Amie and I went to Boston to spend some time with her while I recuperated from my wounds. We ran into a situation that I'm not going to go into with you. You'll have to hear an explanation from Roberta," he exclaimed in a firm voice. "I don't want to hear her name again. I don't want to hear how she's doing or what she's doing. I'll never speak to her again. You can tell her that for me."

"I can't believe we're having this conversation. Are you sure this is what you want? The two of you were meant for each other... What happened?"

"I won't tell you, Bob. I'm never going to give her a chance to do what she did to me again... never. Can you and I still be friends under those conditions? I realize that I'm asking a lot from you. I've valued your friendship more than any man alive."

Bob sat on the chopping block and looked off towards the lake. "I know you well, Evan. Whatever it was that did this to you had to be severe. Are you sure there's nothing I can do to rekindle what you had?"

"No," he replied, unable to hold back the tears.

Bob stood up and embraced Evan in a bear hug just as Joyce stuck her head out the shed door and asked, "Would you two like a cup of coffee? I just took a pan of boulla rolls out of the oven."

"How about it, Evan?" Bob asked, releasing his friend.

Turning away so that Joyce could not see his face, Evan blew his nose nodding. "I'd like that."

Joyce knew that something was wrong and remained silent. She served coffee and sweet boulla rolls, a Finnish and Swedish bread seasoned with cardamom seeds, at her kitchen table. It was her nature not to pry, but she was touched by Evan's look of despair. "Are you all right, Evan? I thought that your wounds were healing well."

Not wanting to elaborate on what he had told Bob, he replied with a hollow smile, "I'm okay, Joyce. My chest still hurts if I twist my body too much, but it's getting less with each passing day. Your boulla rolls are delicious as usual. Of all the foods I missed in France, I dreamed the most about boulla rolls. No one in my outfit knew what I was talking about."

"It was the same in mine," Bob added.

Joyce placed the coffee pot on the table and excused herself to do some ironing in the living room. Evan witnessed the harmony and contentment that ruled in the Gibson home. He had never seen his best friend so happy.

Evan smiled at Joyce, and recalled how she had suffered a horrible loss when they were about six years old. He had left school ahead of Joyce to meet his father in the village where they cashed his check from the quarry and purchased groceries. There had been an accident at the quarry and the whole town was talking about it. Charlie Hammer had been killed when a large slab of slate being lifted from the pit slipped out of its harness, falling on Joyce's father.

Joyce saw Evan in the village and the two of them walked up the hill towards home. They had often done that with Bob and Roberta. Evan learned that Joyce had not heard about her father, and he told her what had happened at the quarry. She ran all the way home crying. It was a terrible thing to do to a friend. Even now, after thirteen years had passed, he felt ashamed that he had blurted out the truth so callously.

The winter of 1921-1922 dragged slowly for Evan. He became more of a recluse than was his natural tendency, fulfilling his game warden duties with more diligence than usual, working sixty to seventy hours a week. When he picked up his mail at the post office, he scanned it for letters from Roberta. Any letters from Roberta were returned to the postmaster with the words "Return to Sender" boldly printed on the envelope.

That spring, Roberta returned home for a few days. Bob had warned Evan of her pending visit, so he placed Amie with his Aunt Mildred and temporarily stayed at the regional headquarters in Greenville so that he could cover a court case. The court session for a person he had arrested for poaching was long in taking place. A guilty verdict was reached mid-day, releasing him. He stopped at his favorite restaurant on a landing at the waterfront. He was tired and hungry, ordering a bowl of fish chowder, a salad, and a cup of coffee. Sitting next to the window with a view of the lake, he watched a plane equipped with floats taxi away from the landing preparing for takeoff. The plane became airborne in a spray of water, turned south and disappeared. The float plane interested him. The ability to land and take off on water had many useful purposes for the Game Warden Service. He made a mental note to bring up the subject with his regional boss, Captain Jim Melee.

Unbeknown to Evan, Roberta Gibson entered the restaurant and scanned the room to locate him. His back was toward the entrance, but she recognized him, and cautiously walked to his booth and took a seat facing him. Her presence shattered his demeanor, filling his consciousness with worrisome questions. Recent images of her and Victor flooded his head with ugly reality he had tried to suppress. She was wearing a blue dress with white lace trim, her hair falling about her shoulders. She was beautiful! He felt trapped and began to slide out of the booth.

She held out her hand to him. "Please, Evan, I need to talk with you," she pleaded.

The waitress served his chowder, asking Roberta if she wanted anything. "Just a coffee, if you don't mind, Evan."

He was speechless and hunched his shoulders in resignation. Unconsciously picking at his salad, Evan said, "I don't have anything to say to you. Your actions told me what you want. It was a brutal message, and I received it loud and clear."

"Would you believe me if I told you it was all a mistake?" The waitress served her coffee.

"No," he replied quickly. "I may be a small town hick, but I'm not stupid. I saw what was taking place. You did it of your own free will. I never violated the trust we shared for a long time. What else is there to say?"

"I understand how badly I treated what we had. I'm sorry... I never meant to hurt you."

"How could it be any other way?" he asked, raising his voice.

She reached across the table, grasping both of his hands in hers. He quickly pulled them away. Her touch sent electric spikes through his body.

"Bob told me that you had been wounded. I've come to ask for your forgiveness," she cried in a wavering voice. "Victor has asked me to marry him. I came home to see if there was anything you and I could do to start over again. No matter what you may think, I still love you."

He had to be careful. It would have been easy for him to have taken her in his arms. Did he really want to lose her forever? Filled with doubts and pain, he lifted his head to look into her blue-green eyes: "If I was to say yes, and it would be easy to forgive, but it would never be the same. Trust has been severely broken and can never be mended as if what took place never existed. I don't believe I could do it. It's over, Roberta. Strange, we thought it was forever, but it lasted only a few years. That's sad. I don't see how we can recapture what we once had. I wish you happiness with Victor. After all, it was a choice you made without any interference from me."

"I understand," she replied, choosing her words carefully. "I was hoping to change your mind, and I was concerned about the severity of your wounds."

"They have healed without a problem. Do you have any idea what a hell it has been these past few months? Combat in France was a piece of cake compared to what you put me through."

"I'm truly sorry, Evan. I really am. I'd give anything to turn the clock back. Are you sure there's no chance for us?"

"To be honest, I'm not sure about anything. Everything has changed, mostly the people. Perhaps we were just too young, and what we thought we had was not so special if you found it that easy to violate. Do you know how hard it is to see you again and not take you in my arms? Then, the image of you in another man's embrace erases everything. I'll never understand why. I can forgive you, but I cannot forget that scene in the hotel room."

Roberta stood up, buttoning her coat. "I'm sorry, Evan. Good-bye." She leaned over and gently kissed him on the lips. Tears streamed down her face as she ran from the restaurant.

He sat alone, stunned by the visit. He knew full well that what he had said was true and for the best, but every nerve in his body urged him to go after her and tell her that they deserved another chance at happiness. She had been his life, his reason for being and now she was walking out of his life forever to another man. Did he really want that?

He left the restaurant and walked along the shore of the lake to his regional headquarters. He was met by an excited Captain Jim Melee. "Evan, we've got a serious situation on our hands. There's a report of a missing plane down."

"What's up, Jim?"

Jim, a heavyset red-headed man with a mellow disposition told Evan that they had received, via the radio, notice of a plane that left Lake Sebago early this morning, destination North Roach Pond at Kokadjo. The party at Kokadjo had contact with the pilot just prior to his departure from Sebago. That was almost six hours ago, and the plane is still missing.

"Wow," Evan exclaimed. "Let's see if the Forest Service plane is still at the lake and available to reconnoiter the area."

Jim pulled on his heavy outer coat. "Okay, let's roll. I've got my Ford. The State Police contacted us that they had a positive sighting of the plane at Spectacle Pond at ten-thirty this morning. No one has seen the plane at Moosehead Lake or Lower Wilson Pond. The plane was carrying three passengers and supplies for Roach Pond."

Just as they pulled into the Forest Service compound, they saw that a float plane was being serviced at the dock. It was an Army surplus plane capable of carrying four people. The pilot, Mike Hancock, told them that he had been briefed on the situation and was ready to patrol the area in question. "The Maine State Police told us that the plane was spotted at Spectacle Pond at about ten-thirty this morning. That leaves an area of about forty miles between Kokadjo, Greenville, and Spectacle. We can assume, for now, that it remained west of Lower Wilson Pond. If both of you come along, you can scan both sides of the grid we'll plot, leaving me to concentrate on flying."

Jim turned to Evan. "Are you sure you're ready for this?"

"Yes, Sir. My chest feels a lot better now. I flew some in the Army."

"Let's go," Jim motioned for the pilot to crank it up.

Once airborne, the pilot flew due east about two miles, then turned south on a track approximately halfway between the main road connecting Monson and Greenville, and Lower Wilson Pond. The sun was still visible in the west, but it was casting some shadows in the forest, making it more difficult to locate a plane that might have crashed. Evan was methodically scanning the terrain on the west side of the plane. The pilot flew low, slightly above stall speed. As they approached Spectacle Pond, Evan spotted a yellow reflection on the ground, motioning for Mike Hancock to circle the area. Closer examination showed a debris field of plane parts and broken trees a hundred feet long.

Evan and Jim desperately focused on the wreckage for any sign of life. There was no movement visible, not a good sign! The closest place to land was a small sliver of shallow water known locally as McLellan Pond. Evan recognized the pond, having checked fishing licenses there one day. Mike traversed the water slowly, searching for any floating logs or debris that might break the fragile pontoons. Seeing none, he set the plane down and coasted toward the western shore about a mile from the crash site. He took a compass bearing to the crash site. "Use an azimuth of due west on a magnetic setting."

Mike shut off the engine and stepped out on the float to check the water. It was only two feet deep. "You were right, Evan. I have some emergency packs we always carry with us. They include blankets and some food, mostly chocolate, tea, and cheddar cheese. You're welcome to both packs. I'll return first thing in the morning with more help. I wish you luck. Most crash scenes are a bad experience. I'll wait here for another hour, giving you time to locate the site. If you determine that a doctor is needed, fire three shots."

"Thanks, Mike," Captain Melee replied, jumping off the float into the water. "Say, do you have an extra flashlight?"

"Oh, yes, you'll need that. All I have is this lantern with a heavy dry cell battery. You're welcome to it." Mike tossed it to Jim.

Evan and Jim instantly struck off on the correct azimuth toward the crash site, pushing as rapidly as they could travel through the thick spruce-fir undergrowth and low-lying swampy area. They were soaked by the time they arrived at the debris field. Three quarters of an hour had passed. They both shouted out to determine if anyone could hear them. There was no response. They quickly dropped their packs and climbed on the broken wing to check the fuselage and cockpit. Evan climbed through a broken window with the lantern. The pilot was dead. He had received a severe blow to the head and chest. The cockpit was filled with blood. The passenger beside the pilot was a young man in his teens. He was also dead.

"Captain, there should be two others in the cargo compartment. The pilot and passenger in the cockpit are both dead."

Climbing over the seat, Evan turned the lantern on the compartment. A woman was wrapped in a blanket, holding a child, also wrapped in a blanket. The child was a boy about two years old. He was staring into the beam of the lantern, frightened and confused. "Are you all right, son?"

"We crashed in the plane," he cried in a high pitched voice.

"Yes, I know. Is this your mother?" he asked, feeling for a pulse.

"I could not wake her up," the boy told him on the verge of hysterics.

"Fire off three shots, Captain. This lady has a bad bruise on the side of her head. She probably has a concussion. Your mother has a pulse, that's encouraging. Are you hurt? If not, would you let my friend, Jim, lift you out of the plane so that I can examine your mother?"

"Come on, young man, we're here to help you. I can get you out of the way. We have some chocolate. Would you like some?" Jim reached to remove him from the compartment.

Evan shined the light about the cubicle, noting the two suitcases and a large duffel bag against which the woman was leaning. That article probably saved the boy and his mother. He carefully stretched the woman's legs out, checking for broken bones. He found none. He dragged her to the rear of the plane so that she was lying flat on the floor. She moaned slightly when he moved her. He was apprehensive about internal injuries. The ugly blue-black bruise on the side of her head and temple were the only visible signs of injury. He checked her eyes. The pupils were dilated, indicating that she was in a coma.

"I found no other injuries, but she's in a coma. We've got to keep her from going into shock. Here's the lantern, Jim. I suggest that we leave the lady where she is until morning. I'll wrap her in another blanket from our packs. This is going to be a long night. How is the boy doing?" Evan asked.

"Aside from being scared to death, he seems to be physically unharmed. He told me his name is Alex. We should build a fire and set up camp for the night." Jim turned the light on the boy. "I have a son about your age. Do you want some chocolate?"

"Yes. Is she going to be all right?" the boy pointed to the woman in the plane.

Evan had been gathering dry dead wood to maintain a fire for the night. He started one using small twigs from fir and spruce and several strips of bark from a white birch tree. Moments after he touched it off with a match, the small pile of twigs burst into flames. He then added larger pieces of dry wood. A fire on a cold night in the Maine woods is like a welcome friend, appreciated by all. The flickering flames illuminated the camp site as well as the dark fuselage where two men met their death. The lady's condition was still unknown. It was a somber scene.

Jim took the lantern and checked the lady in the cargo cubicle. When he shined the lantern on the lady's face, she blinked and turned her head from the light beam. A blink, a good sign! "I'm Captain Melee, a Maine Game Warden. We've arranged for you to be taken out of here tomorrow morning. A doctor will arrive then. Do you understand me?"

She nodded her head and sat up straight. "Where's Alex?" she cried in a weak, desperate voice. "Is he hurt?"

"The young man is outside with my assistant. He's fine except that he's frightened. The pilot and the young passenger did not survive the crash. I'm sorry."

She held her head and wept openly.

"We have a fire outside. It's going to be a cool night. Are you able to climb through this broken window to join us? We can make some hot tea. We have chocolate and cheese if you're hungry, and plenty of blankets to keep you and your son warm," Jim promised.

A few moments later, she stopped crying. "My head hurts and I ache all over my body. I'm not sure if I have any other injuries. I want to get out of this dark box. Please help me."

"Yes, Ma'am. Place your head and shoulders through the window, and I'll lift you out of the plane."

She did as he asked and balanced uncertainly on the ground. "The fire is inviting, thank you."

Jim led her to the fire where Evan already had a can of water from their canteens heating for tea. Evan placed a rubber poncho on the ground beside a yellow birch tree next to the fire. He motioned for her to sit where he folded a wool blanket. She sat on the blanket and rested her head against the tree. He wrapped a blanket around her to keep her from going into shock.

"We have some tea heating on the fire, Ma'am. My name is Evan Mundy, what is yours?"

She lifted her head to look at him, blinking her eyes several times. Flickering shadows from the fire hid parts of his face from her. "Is that you, Sergeant Mundy? I'm Joleen Carpenter."

Chapter Ten

Joleen Carpenter was the last person in the world Evan expected to find in the middle of the wilderness. He was relieved that she was alert and able to move about. Her voice was strained and a little shaky, but he recognized it, and kneeled beside her.

"You've given me the surprise of my life, Joleen." He took a clean washcloth from his pack and wet it before placing it on her bruised forehead. "Hold this on your head. You took a nasty blow. What happened?"

He leaned his head close, for her voice was very weak. She struggled to tell him what took place. "Some friends of mine planned a fishing trip several months ago. They drove up to Roach Pond last week leaving their son, Peter, who was still in school, with me. Alex and I decided to accompany Peter once he had completed school..." She turned to look into the darkened fuselage and began to cry.

Jim remained quiet, listening to Evan and the lady converse. "It's a miracle that you and the child survived. The fact that you and Evan know each other contributes to that miracle."

"This is Joleen Carpenter, Jim. This is my boss, Captain James Melee. Your plane was reported missing. We were lucky to locate you before darkness settled in. We'll have to wait for morning before relief reaches us."

Joleen breathed deeply, wiping the tears from her eyes with her coat sleeve. "The pilot said the engine was missing. Then he screamed that we were going down and to brace ourselves. All I remember is holding on to Alex. I saw limbs swirling around the windows. I was more frightened for Alex than I was for myself."

"The experience is behind you now," replied Evan in a calm, reassuring voice, pouring a hot cup of tea for her. "Here,

71

have some hot tea. It will settle your stomach and warm you. The nights get cold at this time of year in Maine. Alex could handle the tea if he wants to try some."

The four sat around the fire drinking tea and eating chocolate with cheese. The small circle of light emphasized the forbidding darkness that prevailed beyond the flickering flames. The nocturnal animals of the wilderness announced their presence, echoing through the silence of the night. Foxes called to each other in their unique yipping cry, and the eerie sound of owls close to the campsite gave warning to those small mammals that the hunter was close by.

Joleen shared some of her tea with Alex who clung desperately to her. "Thank you for the tea. It does warm the insides."

Evan suddenly stood up to search his jacket pockets, triumphantly holding up two O'Henry candy bars he had recently picked up at the store. "Ah, I had forgotten about these. Would you like to share these with your mother, Alex? I always try to take a few bars with me when hiking in the woods. They not only taste good, they're real nourishing," Evan said triumphantly

Jim watched Joleen and Alex accept the bars and smiled. "I swear you buy those by the case, Evan. I'll get the remaining blankets in the plane so that the two of you can settle down for the night. I'll take the first four hour watch to keep the fire going. You can have the morning shift, Evan."

"That's fine with me," Evan replied.

Darkness blanketed the wilderness, and a solemn silence permeated the campsite, each person alone with their inner self. Evan checked again to be sure that Joleen and Alex were adequately wrapped in their blankets.

He was aware of her grief and discomfort. "I know that it will be a long night for you, Joleen, and that you must hurt all over your body. Try to rest the best you can. If you need anything, just ask us. Good night, old friend."

She turned her tear-filled eyes from the glow of the fire and whispered in a weak voice. "You and Captain Melee have been very kind. Thank you. I'll try to rest. Alex and I will be warm enough in these blankets."

That night Evan curled up in a fetal position on a poncho near the fire. He watched the galaxy of stars overhead, searching for the North Star. It always stayed in the same place where it has guided travelers for centuries. It is the only star in the heavens that maintains the same position throughout the four seasons, and was the seasoned traveler's favorite, giving lost souls an azimuth to follow their own destiny. Its consistency cultivated a sense of security and well-being. Evan called it his best friend in the forest.

Four hours later, Evan took his turn to maintain the fire. Checking his watch, it was almost three in the morning. He poured the balance of the water in their canteens into the metal can for tea and sat with his back against a tree to watch the eastern sky. Slowly, small orange and red plumes of light reflected off the cumulous clouds and began to fill the horizon with a brilliance of color unique to the early winter months of the northeast.

Suddenly, the silence of the forest was broken by the roar of two float planes flying at tree top levels, wagging their wings. Relief was on its way. The planes woke everybody. Evan turned to Joleen to announce: "The first plane out will take you and Alex to the hospital at Greenville. They'll take good care of you. We have time to get warmed up from our last measure of tea before the crews arrive. We'll take the bodies of the pilot and Peter to the funeral home after you and Alex have been cared for."

Within twenty minutes, stretcher bearers arrived at the crash site to carry Joleen and Alex to the waiting planes for transport. Jim and Evan remained behind to make a thorough examination of the plane and the debris field. They had to chop away a portion of the pilot's door to remove the two bodies. It was a grizzly task that either of them would gladly pass if they had the chance. They inventoried the contents of their pockets, leaving the luggage to be checked later once they returned to Greenville.

It was early in the afternoon before they were dropped off at the Forest Service dock. Aunt Mildred and Amie were waiting for them at headquarters. Evan explained to them what had taken place. They had been notified about the crash and were concerned for his safety. Badly in need of a bath and a change of clothes, he suggested that they go back home. He had reports to fill out and promised them he would return home later that evening.

Jim immediately went to the hospital to check on the condition of Joleen and Alex. By the time he returned, Evan was in the barracks shaving. "How are they doing?"

Jim unbuttoned his shirt to take a bath. "The doctor confirmed that she has a concussion. The blows to the side of her head will be painful for a while. She seems to be doing well. Her sister, Aline, was with her and plans to take the child, Alex, back to their cabin at Kokadjo. The doctor wants Joleen to stay at the hospital for a few days for observation. She's lucky to have survived the crash."

Later that evening, after he had completed his reports, Evan reviewed the events of the past few days. His final encounter with Roberta still weighed heavily on his consciousness. Had he been too hasty in dismissing her final plea for reconciliation? His heart ached for that opportunity, but his head warned him that things had changed to the point that they could never recapture the same level of trust and happiness they had once shared.

The innocence that had nurtured their relationship was shattered by the picture of Roberta and Victor Turin together. Forgiveness would have been easy to give, but graphic images would remain forever. Still, he was uncertain if he had made the right decision. Remembering a lifetime of shared experiences with Roberta was not easy to discard. They contributed too many sleepless nights. All of their hopes and dreams had been burned to ashes. Remembrances had an infinite capacity to hurt.

The sudden appearance of Joleen in the Maine wilderness, immediately after his confrontation with Roberta, had only contributed to his discomfort. Now that Jim told him that she had a sister in Kokadjo, he dismissed a visit to the hospital to see her again. His presence might ignite an uncomfortable situation. His vow of silence to Joleen also implied a promise to disappear from the scene. Therefore, rather than visit her, he sent her a bouquet of flowers with a short note...

Dear Joleen,

It was a surprise to see you again under such extreme conditions. I hope and pray that you are doing well and will soon be back with your family. I really wanted to visit you at the hospital to wish you a speedy recovery in person.

Alas, after recalling my promise to you in Washington, I thought it more politic not to take a chance that your family would recognize me. Your son, Alex, has grown since I last saw him. I wish you much happiness and a speedy recovery. I remember so well how you helped countless casualties at the Army hospital.

It was good to see you again. You will always have a very special place in my memory.

Good-bye old friend,

Evan

P.S. Burn this letter after reading.

Several days after the plane crash, Evan picked up Amie at school and headed for home. On their way, he stopped to give a lift to Bob, who was walking home from the quarry. Bob had picked up his mail including a letter from Roberta. He shared its contents with Evan and Amie.

"I feel a little uncomfortable telling you this, Evan, but Roberta and Victor Turin just got married in Boston."

The news was like a physical blow to Evan. His hands gripped the steering wheel of the Ford, turning white. He shook his head. A feeling of despair overwhelmed him. "She told me it was a possibility. I didn't think it would be so soon… What can I say, except wish them much happiness?"

"I've never met the guy," Bob was quick to admit. "She just completed making a new record, *Carolina in the Morning,* and *My Blue Heaven.*"

Evan had purchased four records with eight songs she had already recorded. "Those are pretty songs. I'll look forward to picking them up when they're released. Her voice is better than the last time she sang at the alumni gathering. The full orchestra accompanying her adds to the richness of the sound."

"I wish I could be happier for her success," Bob cried, changing the subject. "Say, are you going to cut wood this weekend? The reason I ask is our neighbor, Pierre Johnson, just finished building me a cordwood scoot. You're welcome to use it if you want."

"I'd like nothing better than adding to my supply of firewood, Bob. If you let me borrow the scoot, I'll help you haul some of your pulpwood out to roadside."

Bob opened the door of the Ford at his home. He laughed at Evan's suggestion. "I was hoping you would help out."

The winter of 1921-1922 passed without incident for Evan and Amie. He had conducted several long patrols, on snowshoes, into the wild areas north of Greenville known as the Allagash Wilderness Waterway. The primary purpose was to observe the condition of the moose and deer population and habitats. Deep snow limited much out-of-door activity except for ice-fishing on the lakes and ponds.

He enjoyed the solitude of the forest, obtaining a peace of mind that allowed him to filter his thoughts and to process impressions of events taking place around him. He had discovered early during his position as a game warden that he was comfortable with the authority that went with the job. He exercised sound judgment administering the State of Maine game laws. His immediate superior, Captain Jim Melee, was impressed with his diligence and sense of fair play. Within the small communities of his patrol responsibilities, he had cultivated a large reservoir of good-will by being his good-natured self.

The position took on more police duties than he expected. The wardens were trained to make arrests and appear in court for the conviction of those who transgressed the laws much like the state and local police officials. He was the only full-time warden in his patrol area, roughly about forty miles around Greenville. None of the towns had policemen except for Greenville. Some towns assigned a local person as a deputy county sheriff. Generally, they were untrained even though many of them performed well in times of emergencies.

Evan embraced the hard-working people in his district. They raised their families to be good Christians, and paid their bills, even though it was a struggle to do so. He was one of them. His position of authority within the community was respected, making his job easier. Every year the state gave him a new Ford automobile to carry out his duties. He drove the faithful vehicle over many roads that were nothing more than wagon tracks to an isolated swamp or pond, or to a recent forest harvesting operation.

One community effort that was enjoyed by all in Monson was the annual winter ice-cutting operation. Most of the men got together on Lake Hebron to cut the thick ice into chunks about two feet by six feet with a motorized scoot-like machine and a large circular saw that was pulled along the ice. Several men pulled the ice-cutting saw along at two feet intervals. The slabs were then loaded on drays and scoots for transportation to several community icehouses throughout the village. Once inside the icehouse, sawdust at least a foot thick was placed around the cakes of ice to preserve them during the hot summer months.

During the summer the ice was cut into smaller pieces for use in the iceboxes all over town. An ice house was located a short distance from Bob's farm. Bob, Evan, and Roberta used to climb up into the ice house in the summer to cool off. Bob and Evan usually had the task of hauling the ice chunks with their horses up the hill to the icehouse. It was brutally exhausting work. Both of them used to brag that they were glad to return to their normal jobs once the icehouse was full. It was a community effort that gave everyone a chance to catch up on local gossip. The Finns and Swedes managed to hold a dance that was well attended.

Evan made special efforts to rope off the area where the ice had been cut. It was a definite hazard to adults or children who might fall into the freezing water. Every parent in the village warned their children to not go near the ice until it had frozen thick enough to walk safely on. Most heeded their parent's wishes. But just in case, he watched the area on a daily basis. If he saw children playing or skating nearby, he warned them of the deadly consequences and requested that they confine their activity close to the village proper.

It was this period when Evan first began to attend the Maine Army National Guard facility at Greenville for monthly training sessions. He retained his original master sergeant rating and was urged by his superiors to attend special training classes that would enhance the possibility of obtaining an officer's commission once an opening became available in the Guard. His war experience in France made him a more effective leader of the younger men assigned to his company. The Maine National Guard traditionally spent two weeks a year training at Fort Drum in New York State, or in New Brunswick performing training maneuvers with Canadian army troops.

Early in the spring of 1922, Evan spent two weeks with his infantry company training with Canadians. He had been a part of the advance elements responsible for locating facilities, purchasing food supplies, and preparation of joint training exercises. It was on this tour of duty that his superiors observed Evan's ability to carry out difficult orders. He was a natural leader who quickly earned the respect of his men. Respect came from the top down, and the men were quick to respond to that fact.

The day the company returned to Greenville, Evan went directly to the game warden headquarters where he met with Captain Jim Melee.

"Ah, the warrior returns. Welcome back, Evan."

"Hi, Jim. It was a fun respite from routine. Those Canadians are good soldiers. I remember in France we relieved a Canadian regiment that held a portion of the line near Paris. They were practically wiped out, but they still held on, giving as good as they received. They had seventy per cent casualties. Their tenacity earned my respect and admiration."

"We share that opinion, Evan. I'm glad you stopped by. You have some mail I placed on your desk along with a schedule of school visits. Take a look at it and let me know how many you can work into your schedule. I've got to run. Lock up after you leave. Oh, by the way, I had your Ford serviced while you were away."

"Thanks, Jim," Evan replied, heading for his desk.

He quickly skimmed through the mail noting several intra-state memos regarding pending and current legislature; forms for his daily time schedule; and several notices of wanted criminals within the state. Near the bottom of the pile was a letter addressed to him. He vaguely recognized the handwriting and quickly opened the letter from Joleen:

Dear Evan,

I've recuperated from my experience in the plane crash. The death of Peter has been especially difficult. His youthful cheerfulness will be missed by all.

I was hoping that you would stop by to see me at the hospital so that I could thank you in person for all that you did. The moment I saw you in the forest I knew that everything would work out. I have to admit the crash was the most frightening experience of my life.

I am returning to Maine this spring and will stop by to say "hello". I'd like to have your opinion about some land I am interested in purchasing.

Wishing you well.

Sincerely,

Joleen

Chapter Eleven

Evan penned a short response to Joleen, telling her that he was looking forward to seeing her again. Late in April, he was ordered to Augusta for two weeks of hearings and training sessions. Amie stayed with Joyce and Bob, her Aunt Mildred had a bout with the flu.

Part of Evan's refresher course was a lecture and discussion of new legislative enactments pertinent to the wildlife and forests of the state. He was pleased to learn that the Legislature had increased funding to the Game Warden Service. Two new aircraft and a few pilots were funded to assist in administration, research, and patrol work. The planes would be most helpful in search and rescue operations which was taking more and more of their time and energy.

Prior to returning to Monson, he checked several record shops for Roberta's most recent recordings. He found the latest release to be *Bye Bye Blackbird,* and on the reverse side, *Night and Day.* The first time he heard them at the store, the sound of her voice overwhelmed him with sadness. She was wonderful. Her voice was the best he had heard it. Her renditions of the ballads touched his fragile peace of mind. It appeared that his Roberta was making a name for herself!

She had been featured on a national radio network with Paul Whitman's band. He called her one of the best female vocalists in the country. Evan had all he could do to control the tears that welled in his eyes. The sudden rush of emotion shattered his complacency, and that angered him.

When he returned to Monson, via the Bangor and Aroostook Railroad, he stopped to pick up Amie at Bob's and Joyce's place. He shared the recordings with them, and left shortly after. The songs touched a very private part of his inner feelings, and he was not in a mood to discuss them with his two best friends, or allow them to see how the music affected him.

One day in May, Evan was busy taking readings at the weather station beside the headquarters building in Greenville. He measured daily rainfall, wind velocity, relative humidity, and recorded it in his daily log. Jim called to him that he had a visitor. Thinking that it might be the department attorney stopping by to go over current court cases, he was surprised to see Joleen Carpenter sitting in his conference room.

"Hello, stranger," he greeted her, offering his hand. "It's nice to see you again."

She was dressed in warm clothes suitable for the out-of-doors, looking lovely as usual. She had that familiar smile he remembered so well from the hospital. "I was hoping to see you today, Evan. You're looking well. The Maine woods seem to agree with you."

"I'm a lucky man," he replied. "I get paid to do a job I'd do for a lot less. Sometimes the hours are long and demanding, but Amie and I adapt, thanks to generous friends and family. You look a lot better than the last time I saw you, Joleen." He checked his pocket watch, and asked, "Could I treat you to a lunch?"

She smiled, "That would be nice. I don't want to interfere with your work. I understand that the Maine wardens are a very active and efficient group."

Jim Melee stuck his head through the door, greeting Joleen. He had visited her in the hospital just before she was discharged. "I hope you've recovered from your ordeal, Miss Carpenter."

She turned to him and replied, "Oh yes, thanks to you two dedicated wardens."

"Captain," Evan said. "I just invited Miss Carpenter to lunch. If you don't mind, I'll take the rest of the day off. I'll make that Little Wilson Stream patrol shortly."

"Evan, you work too hard. Take the weekend off, you've earned it. It has been nice seeing you again, Miss Carpenter."

"Thanks, Captain," Evan replied.

"My automobile is in the parking lot," she said, following Jim out the door, pointing to a dark green 1921 Hupmobile closed sedan. "I just received my driver's license."

Evan admired the vehicle, opening the driver door for her. "Wow. What a pretty sedan. This is the first Hupmobile I've ever seen."

"My father claimed that they made one of the best engineered automobiles for the money. My entire family has taken his wise advice and found them to be very dependable."

"My favorite restaurant is at Greenville Junction, just past the hospital, on the waterfront. They make the best custard pies in the area," he chuckled.

Joleen was silent, paying attention to her driving and shifting gears. "The family kept all of the papers that featured the plane crash," she mentioned without comment.

He was concerned that his name was mentioned in most of the accounts he had read. If her family members picked up on that, then his role as Joleen's husband must have been questioned. "I've been afraid for that. It was one of the reasons I did not visit you at the hospital."

She answered him in a hesitant voice. "That was one of the things I wanted to discuss with you."

He noted the sober tone. "Where is Alex?"

"He's with my sister in Virginia. You must know that my sister and her husband have a cabin on First Roach Pond."

"Yes," he replied, pointing to the right. "Turn here across the railroad tracks. The restaurant is straight ahead on the waterfront."

She parked the Hupmobile, and they entered the restaurant, taking a seat next to the water with a grand view of the lake. They ordered clam chowder and coffee. Evan suggested that if she wanted to order wine or a cocktail, he did not object. Since he was in uniform he chose not to drink alcoholic beverages in public.

She smiled. "I'm not a drinker, Evan. Coffee will be fine. You must be anxious to know what I have to share with you."

"To be honest, I am eager to hear what you have to say. The charade we carried out has been bothering me for a long time, especially since your plane crash. Prior to that I was able to live with it and to let it be history. Now, it has become complicated. A lot has happened to me since then. Adjusting to a life without my parents has not been easy for me or Amie, who has been a blessing to me. I take my responsibility for her

82

seriously, and she is supportive of most everything I do. At times though, I'm frightened of the obligation."

"She reached across the table and squeezed his hands in hers. "I'm sure you're a wonderful big brother. If I remember correctly, you were very close to a school classmate; I don't recall her name."

Evan looked out at the lake, avoiding her discerning glance. The lines around his mouth hardened. "Roberta Gibson and I were engaged to marry. When I found that she was unfaithful to our commitment, I walked away without looking back. I have no regrets about that decision. End of conversation, Joleen."

She saw the pain he was still carrying and quickly apologized. "I'm so sorry for you, Evan. You deserved better. I didn't mean to pry into your private life. I had no right. Forgive me."

The waitress brought them fresh yeast rolls, coffee, and steaming hot clam chowder. Eager to change the subject, Evan tasted the chowder. "Ah, it's one of my favorite meals. Whenever I'm near the coast I splurge on clam chowder and steamed clams."

"It is delicious," she replied. "I had several reasons for making this trip. One was to release you from your vow of secrecy. It does not matter now. It was intended to shield my father from the truth that would only hurt him. Because he had been so fragile for a long time, the family was afraid it would be too much for him to handle. Now that he is gone, we can discuss the charade openly. All of my family was aware of what was taking place."

"You don't know how relieved I am to hear those words. I've had a guilty feeling ever since that boat trip down the Potomac. Where is Alex's real father?"

It was a simple question, but it caught Joleen off balance. It required an answer she was unprepared to give. Her eyes opened wide, avoiding him. "He is no longer around. We separated long before Alex was born. He wants no part of the child and refuses to acknowledge parenthood."

"Do you still love him?" Evan asked.

"No," she quickly answered. "It was an infatuation that got out of control and was soon over. Do you think less of me for having been so careless?"

"I'm not in any position to judge you, or anyone else, Joleen. The war years affected everybody differently. I formed a very positive opinion of you by your performance at the hospital. Your personal life belongs to you, alone." He watched a plane take off the water. "Now, what else did you want to tell me? I can't believe that you drove all this distance just to chat with me."

She soberly replied, "Don't sell yourself short, Evan. I came to seek your advice on a piece of land I want to buy. You are as knowledgeable as anyone about the forestland in this portion of Maine. When we are finished eating, I'd like to show you the parcel I have in mind. My father has been very generous in his will to his remaining family. I want to invest some of my inheritance in land. I chose northern Maine because our family has visited here often over the years. I love the vastness and the serenity of the wilderness."

Admiring her appreciation for the land, Evan smiled at her reaction to his question. "That sounds like a great idea, Joleen. I'll be glad to give you my opinion for what its worth. However, I'd advise you to seek the advice of a professional forester before making a final decision."

"I was planning to do that," she answered, grasping his hands across the table. "I also made the trip to say thank you to an old friend who has helped me out at two different times in my life when I really needed it."

"I've thought often about our trip down the Potomac. Thanks for releasing me of my vow of silence. I'm glad that things have worked out for you. I'm ready to leave after we have another cup of coffee and a piece of custard pie, the best in Maine."

"That sounds wonderful. I dressed for a walk in the woods."

A half hour later, they were parked beside Little Wilson Pond where a rowboat was tied to a small dock. Evan was familiar with the pristine body of water. "I've been lucky enough to explore the shore lines around this isolated pond. The views are spectacular from the hills on the eastern shore."

She opened the rear door of the Hupmobile and removed a painting she had made of the area. "This is an oil painting I did last year from memory."

He recognized the prominent elevation, known locally as Rum Mountain that rose precipitately from a snug cove. She had painted a small log cabin on a flat location near the summit of the mountain. "Your painting is very good. Is the cabin a part of your interest in the area?"

"Yes," she answered, replacing the painting in the back seat of the automobile. "We can row across to the cove and pick up a trail I've marked with patches of white linen."

"I'm anxious to see what you have in mind. You set the pace and I'll follow. I'll row us across to the cove. Do you paint much?"

"Landscapes are my favorite," she replied, setting a brisk pace down the knoll to the boat. "This area of Maine with its isolated bodies of water and rugged terrain have always fascinated me. I paint as often as I can. I have several pencil sketches just crying to be completed."

This quiet and unassuming lady was full of surprises. Her interest in the vast Maine wilderness set her apart from many of the wealthy socialites she must have grown up with. Evan helped her into the boat and rowed the short distance to a rocky shore where he noted a white flag tied to a bramble bush blowing in the wind.

The sheer cliffs appeared to be inaccessible. She pointed to a pathway she had flagged and triumphantly led him to the small plateau where she had placed the cabin in the painting. They sat on a granite ledge and admired the view to the west with Moosehead Lake and Kineo Mountain in the background. Much of Little Wilson Pond was visible in the foreground.

"This is as good as it gets," he cried enthusiastically. "Do you own this parcel of land, Joleen?"

"Not yet," she replied, breathing heavily from the rugged climb. "This is part of the Bowdoin College Grant who does not look kindly on any type of development. My father was a graduate of the college and has made generous donations to it over the years. I cannot purchase the land, but I have permission to build a seasonal log cabin on this spot. The college will retain ownership of land and cabin, with me as primary occupant. I cannot sell it or rent it. What do you think, Evan?"

He sat on the ledge beside her, admiring the panoramic view. "I don't blame you for being attracted to the area. My only concern would be the engineering problems in building a cabin on these granite formations. There is no adequate place for a septic system or a well without drastic alterations to the area, which the college board may strenuously object to. To be honest, its location is fantastic for its views, but a little remote for easy access. Use in the winter after snowfall would be dangerous. Am I dampening your enthusiasm?"

She shook her head. "No, I wanted your honest opinion. You gave that to me, Evan. I was thinking of a hideaway to retreat to when the bustle of city life becomes too burdensome. Perhaps I have been overpowered by the view."

"I'm sure that there are plenty of isolated places available with better access any time of the year," Evan mused, seeing the disappointment on her face. "I know of a place that is isolated and still accessible by automobile near a bubbling stream with a view of Boarstone Mountain. I know the family that owns several hundred acres of land around the site. We can check it out tomorrow if you're interested."

"Where is it located?" she asked.

"It's east of Monson at the junction of Little Wilson and Big Wilson Rivers. I've hunted and fished the area several times with my father. It's too late to travel there before dark. I expect that tomorrow will be fair weather," he smiled. "Collecting meteorological data gives me an inside track on weather forecasting."

She jumped off her seat on the granite ledge. "That sounds interesting. I'll take you back to Greenville. I was planning to stay at my sister's place in Kokadjo for the night."

He noted her hesitation. "I've got to pick up Amie at our neighbor's. You're welcome to stay with us for the night. Amie will be thrilled for the company. I give you my word that your reputation will not be compromised. We have fixed up my parents' bedroom for guests, which should be comfortable. I'll even put on my chef's hat and cook supper."

She smiled at him. "How can a person refuse such a gracious offer?"

"We can leave your Hupmobile at the headquarters overnight and take my Studebaker to Monson. I'll bring you back there tomorrow. My boss, Jim, has been after me to take more time off. It has been a pleasant respite being with you again, Joleen."

Joleen climbed out of the rowboat onto the trail leading to her automobile where she paused to look back at the mountain scene she had so eagerly shown to Evan. He saw the wistful expression and felt guilty that he had been so negative.

"Are you angry that I did not reinforce your impressions of the location? I'm flattered that you sought my opinion."

She nimbly stepped over several rocks on the path and replied, "Don't feel bad. I can accept your practical evaluation of the site. My eagerness for the view blanked out all other aspects of the site. The first time I visited the site was shortly after my father passed away. I had a feeling that he was with me while I was there. My attachment was personal and emotional… The place you describe sounds fascinating."

They remained silent climbing the path to her automobile. She had shown him a sentimental side of herself and he felt uncomfortable that he had let her down. He opened the driver's door for her and saw her moist eyes.

"I'm sorry, Joleen," he whispered, placing a finger under her chin, gently kissing her.

Chapter Twelve

Evan and Joleen parked her Hupmobile at the headquarters building, picking up his Studebaker for the ride back to Monson. They were both in a reflective mood, evaluating their response to the impromptu embrace at Wilson Pond. As they passed Spectacle Pond, he pointed out to her where he had arrested a poacher a few days ago. He remarked that it had been a classmate of his in Monson Academy.

"I really regretted having to arrest a friend. He came from a poor family much like all the rest of us in town. I knew they could use the meat to feed their family. I would have walked away from the location and said nothing, but he had two other men with him that recognized me. I had no alternative. I plan to see that the court is lenient on him when his case is heard."

She was not surprised that the arrest bothered him. "The State of Maine is well served by your dedication and sound judgment. Laws need to be interpreted with wise council. It's nice that you take that responsibility seriously."

He blushed at the compliment. "There are those who would disagree with you."

They entered the main street of Monson where he proudly pointed out the schools that he had attended. He also told her about his encounter at the local drug store where he was caught stealing candy. His enthusiasm in telling the tale made her smile. She saw the little boy side of his serious demeanor.

He turned to the left onto Depot Street to pick up Amie at Uncle Del's and Aunt Mildred's place. It was a neat, recently painted New England style house with a steep pitched roof to shed snow. Amie had seen the automobile and ran across the porch, excited to see her brother again.

"Hi, Amie. We have a surprise guest for the evening, Miss Joleen Carpenter. Joleen, this is my sister, Amie. She just turned twelve this past winter."

Joleen opened the passenger door to let her in the Studebaker. "I'm pleased to meet you, Amie. Your brother had told me a lot about you." They shook hands as Amie climbed into the back seat.

Aunt Mildred stepped out on the porch to wave to them. "Uncle Del is away on a fishing expedition with a party from New York," Amie told them, quietly evaluating the young lady sitting beside her brother.

"Miss Carpenter is the lady who was in the plane crash. It was quite a coincidence; I had met her in the Army hospital where I was recovering from my wounds," Evan explained, waving to Aunt Mildred.

"Are you a nurse, Miss Carpenter?" Amie asked, examining her closely.

"No, Amie. I was a volunteer worker helping out where I could. It was a wonderful experience. No one can imagine the heroism that takes place in the wards of the hospital. It made me appreciate the sacrifices of so many brave men."

"I'm going to be a nurse," Amie announced.

"This is the first time I've heard this from you, Amie. That's wonderful. Next year you'll be a freshman in high school. You'll want to take all the science courses you can." He smiled at her in the rear view mirror. "I promised Miss Carpenter that we'd prepare supper. Do you have any suggestions?"

"Well, Aunt Mildred gave me a jar of spaghetti sauce she just made. It's in my bag. How about spaghetti and warmed over boulla rolls?"

"You heard the suggestion, Joleen, what do you say? You're our guest of honor."

"Spaghetti sounds wonderful. What are boulla rolls?" she asked.

Amie and her brother chuckled at the question. Amie was quick to tell her about the sweet roll. It was a staple item in the homes of the Finnish and Swedish families that made up a large part of the inhabitants in the town of Monson. Evan told her that outside of the village, few people had ever heard of the delicacy. They all laughed that it was treasured in Monson and introduced to summer tourists every year.

The house was cool when they first entered the kitchen. Evan quickly built and lit a fire in the large cast-iron cook stove and in the fireplace in the living room. A fire felt good as soon as the sun had set. Amie was anxious to show Joleen the rest of the house.

Their parents' master bedroom on the second floor was her favorite. It was a large room with soft blue flower wallpaper on the walls. It had a large balcony over the woodshed that connected to the barn. The view of the lake shortly after sunset with fading rays of red and orange flashing against the mirror-smooth water of Lake Hebron was beautiful. The room had an air of warmth and serenity that Joleen felt as soon as she entered the bedroom.

"This is a wonderful room, Amie," she remarked, surprised at how comfortable she felt. After all, she was a stranger in a strange place, yet she did not feel unwelcome. She noted a picture of their mother and father on the bureau. They reflected the dignity and integrity of hard-working parents. Her first impression upon viewing the portrait for the first time was how lucky Evan and Amie were to have been nurtured in such a caring environment, a treasured legacy of selflessness. Joleen envied them.

She recalled her own life with two parents who obviously loved her and her sister, Aline. Their economic status purchased everything they ever wished for. Joleen in particular yearned for a closer, warmer relationship she never had with her mother. It had been different with her father, whom she loved dearly for his warmth and compassion. She would have gladly traded her rather exclusive existence for the simpler environment Amie and Evan had been blessed to share. She envied the emotional security that grew out of such a rich home life.

That evening Joleen retired early to the spacious bedroom. Her head was filled with thoughts of tomorrow. Her spontaneous decision to seek Evan's advice about land she wanted to purchase gave her pause to closely examine why?

She was pleased to release him from his vow of secrecy in the hope that it removed some of the distaste she knew accompanied the deceitful act. Joleen had just turned off the lamp beside the bed when she was treated to the melancholic sounds of whippoorwills calling to each other just outside the windows. It was a melancholic sound that touched her, leaving her with an empty feeling she could not explain. Here, far away from the hectic pace of everyday life in the larger cities, she found peace and serenity at the edge of the vast Maine wilderness. Her frequent visits to the area had ignited a deep longing to own a part of that rich natural heritage she could call her very own.

Sleep did not come easy to Joleen. She reviewed over and over the old question of where do I go from here? Vivid thoughts of a recent conversation with a young man she had known most of her life still troubled her. Steven Hadley was a successful lawyer in Washington and a frequent visitor to the Carpenter home. He had been associated with her father on some of his business dealings. She had occasionally gone out on dates with him, but had never seriously thought of him as anything but a friend.

Steven had always been quite inquisitive about anything pertaining to the Carpenter family, without divulging anything about his own life. She dismissed his searching mind as part of what made him such a good lawyer. As she got to know him better, she found him to be manipulative and controlling of people and events around him. She had him pegged as a phony and avoided him whenever possible. He enjoyed impressing people with his ability to function at the top of the social scene in Washington. Those who traveled within the hierarchy of the very active social structure were his idols.

He had helped to prepare Joleen's father's will. Therefore, he was aware of her father's full estate and of the amount each family member was to receive. Joleen's share of the estate was much greater than her sister Aline or her mother. It could have been cause for a family feud, so Joleen hired an accountant to administer her estate and to divide it so that the estate was shared evenly.

A short time after Joleen's father died, Steven had approached her for a loan of several thousand dollars so that he could take advantage of a scheme that would make him rich. She flatly refused him the money and an offer to accompany him to Los Angeles for a week. Up to that time, he had paid little attention to her. The more she saw of him, the more she disliked and distrusted his motives. The two refusals triggered an explosive response from him. He went into a tirade, explaining that he knew that she could afford it, and he desperately needed it. She calmly told him again that her answer was still no. Her funds were all tied up and being administered by an accountant.

Steven started to swear, calling her vile names. She was afraid that he was going to hit her. His parting statement left her frightened, loathing him for his despicable conduct: "Oh, you and those like you who think you're so high and mighty and perfect. I know all about the filthy game you and the family carried out for your father's sake. For your information, he knew all about it, and I was the one to tell him..."

The fact that Steven might have known about the cruise on the yacht was unlikely, unless he had bribed some of the crew members... His rage had left her exhausted and angry at her vulnerability. Since then she had been experiencing sleepless nights, wondering what his vindictive rage would produce.

Joleen awoke from a restful night's sleep to the tantalizing aroma of fresh coffee percolating downstairs. She freshened up with the water pitcher and washbowl on the stand next to the bed and hurried downstairs where Evan was tending the fire in the black cook stove.

He heard her descending the steps. "Good morning, Joleen."

"The smell of coffee was a powerful incentive to get out of bed," she grinned at him. "Is there anything I can do to help?"

"Well," Evan turned from the stove to look at her, relieved that the long lines around her eyes and mouth were gone. "I hope you rested well. The whippoorwills can be a nuisance at times."

"Oh, no. They were wonderful. They helped me to relax. I did sleep soundly."

"What do you like for breakfast?" he asked. "We have eggs and ham if you want them. Our neighbor just brought over a fresh batch of boulla rolls. They're a natural with coffee."

"Just one of your famous boulla rolls and a cup of coffee will be fine," she told him, taking a seat at the large kitchen table next to him. "How long have you been up, Evan?"

"I'm an early riser. Old habits die hard. I like getting up just before the sun rises out of the east. It's a time when the whole world seems to be at peace with itself. I got the fire started, and fed and watered the horse in the barn. Amie usually sleeps a couple more hours except for school days." He set out two cups of coffee and took a tin of rolls from the pantry behind the stove. "Help yourself, Joleen."

"I take my coffee black without cream or sugar. You're a very gracious host. The room I slept in was filled with peaceful energy. I could feel it as soon as I entered the room. I've never experienced anything like it in my life. I had the feeling that your mother and father were watching over me," she exclaimed.

Evan was silent for a while, pondering her words. "You know," he replied with a sober tone, "I've had that same feeling since I first came home from the hospital. There are times when I feel their presence close to me, and I share some little thing with them, then I realize that they are really gone... I still miss them; and pray that they're guiding me. Sometimes I feel lost and unsure of what is expected of me. I never realized how much I depended on their judgment until I came home to find the house empty."

"I did not mean to dredge up old memories, Evan," she said. "These boulla rolls are delicious. I understand your addiction to them." She laughed to lighten up the reflective atmosphere.

For almost two hours they sat at the table drinking coffee and discussing land values and its availability. He asked her why she wanted forest land and if she anticipated moving away from Washington, or if she wanted a seasonal place to use as a retreat, like many summer places in the area. She confided in him that her father had been a close friend of Clifford Pinchot for years. He was considered the father of American forestry. She and her father shared his passion for the land and the concept of sustainable forest products attainable from professionally managed forestlands.

She had read much of the current literature about the subject and was enthusiastic about forestland as an investment as long as they were professionally managed to increase quality and productivity of the available growing stock. The concept of "sustained yield" fascinated her. If she could combine sound stewardship with the opportunity to reside within the forest tract, it would be the culmination of all the hopes and dreams she held for the project, even if her residence was only seasonal.

She had given the project a lot of thought, mused Evan. She was even more knowledgeable of forest management practices than he was aware. He knew of the large tract of land he had intended to show to her. It had the potential of yielding an annual allowable harvest of several hundred cords of spruce and fir pulpwood per year. At one spot on the property, he mentioned an awesome view existed at the juncture of the Big Wilson River and the Little Wilson River, with Boarstone Mountain in the background.

He described the parcel of land to her and offered to take her out there in his Studebaker. Amie was pleased to tag along, enjoying the company of the soft-spoken Joleen.

About ten miles northeast of Monson on a bumpy dirt road, Evan took them to a spot where Little Wilson flowed into the larger Big Wilson in a deep granite-walled chasm strewn with large rock outcrops. The churning flume could be heard for a long distance away. The power of the two bodies of water mixing together in a boiling mass of unleashed energy swirled and smashed their way through the slabs of granite in the ravine. A steady mist of churned water rose from the cauldron, creating its own micro-climate that was much cooler than the surrounding territory. The relentless drive of the water through the chasm shook the immediate ground. It's a phenomenon that affects every individual and touches all of the human senses: emotional, physical, and audible.

Any person lucky enough to experience the site never forgets its powerful impact. It becomes an instant reality check for man. Compared to nature's unleashed forces, man's place on earth seems insignificant and fragile in comparison.

Evan had viewed the scene several times from a vantage point close to the roadway. Each visit created the same inspiring sensation to his senses. He watched Joleen's reaction closely. Her mood instantly changed from a talkative potential buyer of the property to a silent pensive observer. Amie was also excited and a little frightened by the thundering volatility below them.

The scene is one of contrasts. At first, one becomes quiet and respectful almost like entering a church. Idle chatter

94

seems out of place. Awe and admiration for a God capable of creating such a powerful demonstration of His powers is a humbling experience. Yet, the boiling mass of water could be dangerous and deadly to those who did not take precautions. The river's ruthlessness is a manifestation of its incessant adherence to the laws of gravity and the route of least resistance.

Joleen was mesmerized by the site, remaining sober and contemplative for several minutes, studying the area. Later, they walked over portions of the forest tract where Evan pointed out some of the surveyed boundary lines. They rested a few minutes, sitting down on a granite outcrop. Joleen looked up to study Boarstone Mountain's massive formation which dwarfed everything around it.

Evan broke the silence first. "What do you think, Joleen?"

She turned to look at him, "I don't know when I've been moved by anything like the two rivers colliding with each other. Words fail me to describe it, but I can tell you with certainty that I want to buy the property. Places of beauty like this should be available for everyone to experience. If I can buy it, I'll see to it that it's available to those who wish to visit." She was breathlessly excited about the prospect. "Thank you for showing it to me, Evan."

"I had a feeling you'd like it." Her enthusiasm for the tract exceeded his expectations. "Amie and I have fished both streams above and below the juncture. It's one of my regular patrols. The rapids have always given me a sensation of peace, wellness, and thanksgiving."

"Oh, yes, it does have that kind of power," she exclaimed, jumping off the rock. Suddenly, she was hesitant and looked up at Evan, who was still sitting on the ledge. "I don't need to look at any more of the land right now. I've been thinking about something that has been on my mind for a long time. Would you mind taking me back to Greenville to pick up my Hupmobile? Then you could follow me to my sister's cabin at Kokadjo. There's something that needs to be settled, and now is as good a time as any."

"What do you mean, Joleen?"

"Please, don't ask me to explain just now," she soberly replied. "You'll understand everything soon, dear friend, so bear with me."

Evan shrugged his shoulders and jumped off the ledge. "Whatever you want, Joleen. By the way, what do you say if we have lunch at Greenville?" he asked, perplexed at the sudden turn of events.

"I'd like that," she smiled. "The custard pie was delicious."

Two hours later, they were at Joleen's sister's cabin at Roach Pond. They had enjoyed a good meal at Greenville and proceeded to Kokadjo in both vehicles. Evan was apprehensive and did not know what was going to happen. He noticed two fine Buick sedans with New York license plates parked in the driveway.

Joleen pulled her Hupmobile into the drive first, quickly getting out of the vehicle and walking back to Evan and Amie. "This is my sister's cabin. Aline and my mother arrived today for a visit. Little Alex is with them." She saw a puzzled look on Evan's face and reached out for his hand. "Come, Evan, I do this more for you than for anyone else. You come along too, Amie."

As soon as they entered the cabin, Alex recognized Joleen and ran into her open arms. She picked him up and introduced him to Amie and Evan. "You may remember Mr. Mundy. He helped us get out of the plane crash."

"I remember you well, Alex," Evan said, holding out his right hand to the young man.

"I remember you," he said, taking Evan's hand in his. He then looked at Amie, a stranger.

Evan saw the look, "This is my sister, Amie."

"Hi, Alex," she cheerfully answered.

Joleen's mother entered the great room of the cabin from a room off to the left. Joleen ran to embrace her. "It's nice to see you again, Mother. You remember Evan, and this is his sister Amie."

Mona Carpenter was dressed in a colorful plaid shirt with a long blue skirt. Her blond hair was pulled in a coiled bunch at the back of her head. She was an attractive woman with an independent air of self-sufficiency. She warmly welcomed Evan and Amie to the cabin.

"It's nice to see you again, Mrs. Carpenter," Evan shook her hand, feeling uneasy.

Joleen witnessed his uneasiness and suggested that they sit out on the deck where they could be comfortable. Mrs. Carpenter told them that Aline had taken the canoe out for a tour of the pond. At that moment, Alex asked if he could walk along the edge of the water. Evan suggested that Amie might accompany him. She liked being with children and was glad to get away from the rather heavy atmosphere that existed with the adults.

Mona Carpenter took a seat directly in front of Evan and Joleen, who sat beside him. "This is not an easy time for me or my mother. You must know, Mother, that I have told Evan all about our deception with father. That is past and hopefully will be forgotten by all concerned. We all pray for dear father's forgiveness. I have released Evan from his vow of secrecy, and now, we must be honest with him and tell the whole truth."

Evan could feel the tension in the room. He looked at Mrs. Carpenter who had tears in her eyes. She wiped them away with a handkerchief. She saw his puzzled look. "We owe you an explanation, Evan Mundy. My daughter, Joleen, has carried a heavy burden of guilt with grace and unbelievable dignity. She has asked me to free her of that commitment she so selflessly assumed to protect my husband. I love her dearly for her loyalty, strength, and courage."

"I don't understand, Mrs. Carpenter."

She blew her nose and continued: "I owe all of you an apology. Alex is not Joleen's son. He is mine."

Chapter Thirteen

Evan drove slowly back to Monson. Mona Carpenter's heartfelt confession of her transgressions had touched him. She claimed that she had visited several hospitals filled with wounded soldiers and sailors throughout the western part of the country during the war. At one in particular, she was attracted to a young Army surgeon. The attraction had been mutual and resulted in several clandestine trysts. Shortly after their affair, he was transferred to France. Several months before the surrender, he was killed in an artillery barrage.

Mona Carpenter was left with positive evidence of her unfaithfulness. Her husband's health began to deteriorate at about the same time, adding to her anguish and shame. She was determined to keep the pregnancy from him, hoping to place the child up for adoption after it was born. She had often taken extended trips about the country handling some of the family business affairs, and she used that as an excuse to hide her obvious pregnancy from her husband. It was during this period that the family unanimously decided on the plan that included Evan to hide the truth from Joleen's father.

Evan had left the cabin with Amie, saddened and disappointed that such a lovely lady as Joleen's mother could so easily and deceitfully violate her marriage to such a fine man as her husband. It was obvious that she was saddened and ashamed of her actions. He was more than willing to forgive and forget that he had been a part of the scandalous act. Now was the time to put the past to rest.

The weekend he had spent with Joleen had brought back many of the same feelings he had entertained watching her function in the hospital wards. The sham they had played on her father was good enough to convince him they were married. Evan knew then it would be easy to love this gentle unassuming lady. Returning as he did to pick up his life where he had left it with Roberta had pushed aside the secret undeclared yearnings he harbored for Joleen. Seeing her at the plane crash had released those suppressed emotions he thought he had successfully cast aside.

He recalled with a warm glow the few moments they spent saying good-bye at her sister's cabin at Roach Pond. She had promised to evaluate the property they had visited and thanked him for a pleasant weekend. "I must say you handled my mother's situation with tact and grace. Thank you for being so understanding. Please forgive me for making you a part of this sordid affair. I wanted to bring it all out into the open so that you and I could remain friends."

"You know," he had answered, looking at the moonlight reflecting on the water. "I was not surprised to learn that Alex was her son. She had that look about her whenever she picked him up on the yacht. You never seemed as passionate with him as she did, and that fact bothered me a little."

"Looking back on the episode, I wish we had handled it differently. Poor father, I still feel badly that I lied to him. We were very close. I'd have done anything not to hurt him..."

"From what I remember of him, I'm sure that he looks upon your intentions and forgives you, Joleen. Your mother may be treated differently, but that's not for me to judge." He placed an arm around her waist. "It has been a nice weekend with you. Will I see you again?"

She turned to him and asked softly, "Do you want that?"

The question surprised him, making him unsure what she expected of him. "I'm a believer in straight talk, Joleen. You've been in my thoughts, almost on a daily basis, since I left the hospital. However, I've tried to be realistic. You and I live in different worlds and travel in different social circles. I'm uneducated and lack the sophistication and the ability to provide those nice things that surround you. What I'm trying to say, and I know I'm saying it badly, is I'm a poor country boy, and you are a very lovely wealthy lady. I simply can't compete with those who have more to offer..."

She placed a finger to his lips. "Hush, Sergeant Mundy. What has money or position got to do with affairs of the heart? If money could purchase happiness, then the wealthy would be the happiest people on the planet. Trust me, that is not the case. When you returned to the hospital after our Potomac expedition, my father and I had time to share many things. He knew he was dying. He was touched by the values which are a large part of the wonderful person you are. He was wealthy and very generous to those he loved; yet, he remained a modest, caring person all his life. The family loved him dearly for his unpretentiousness."

"What are you trying to say, Joleen?"

"I've fallen in love with you, Evan," she whispered in his ear and kissed him.

Her simple declaration and warm lips struck him like a bolt of lightning, gladdening his heart. They embraced there at the edge of the water glistening under the full moon. Tears slowly formed in Joleen's eyes.

He kissed both eyes and confessed, "I've loved you from a distance, for a long time, knowing that it might never be possible. Every soldier in the hospital was in love with you, Joleen. I was one of them."

That evening they discovered the sheer joy of loving someone special, and being loved in return. Together, they were empowered to take on the world. Possibilities were endless.

Amie interrupted his reverie. She had witnessed what had taken place between her big brother and Joleen. "The last time Roberta was home, Joyce and Bob thought that there was a chance the two of you might settle your differences. I really like Joleen. She's fun to be with and is much quieter than Roberta used to be. Is this a little sudden, Evan?"

"You're an intuitive young lady, Amie. I don't think it's sudden. Actually I've known Joleen for quite a while. Long enough to find out what kind of person she is. I'm glad you like her. She has a gift of making people feel good."

"Since you came home from the war, you haven't smiled much. It was nice to see you laugh and joke this weekend. I think Joleen is good for you, and I like that about her. It's good that someone else sees you the way I do. I'm proud of you, Evan."

He reached across the seat to grasp her hand. "I don't know what I'd have done without you, Sis. By the way, I spoke to your sixth grade teacher, Miss LeClair, the other day. She said you were doing very well with your school work. She told me that you have a natural talent for writing. One of your

English essays was one of the best she had ever read. I had her in the sixth grade, so she's experienced a lot of papers. I was pleased to hear that. I remember how Mom used to have that intense involved look when she was playing the piano. I've seen that same look on you when you've been writing in your notebook."

"Miss LeClair suggested that I start a daily diary or a journal to write about those things that interested me. I find that it helps me sort things out. Music never appealed to me like it did to Mom and you. Expressing my feelings on paper comes easy," she confessed.

"The creative spirit works in different ways for each of us. I encourage you to continue with your personal journals. If you need some notebooks, just let me know. Don't feel guilty about wanting to be alone at times, Amie. I've often seen that part of you; all of us have a similar need. So if sometimes you really just want to be quiet, and I'm being a pest, just tell me to bug-off, and I'll know what you mean."

She laughed with him, laying her head against him. Brother and sister had attained that level of intimacy where they were acutely aware of what each was thinking. It was an empowering moment for them that brought them closer than ever together.

The summer of 1922 brought more tourists to the area. A larger number than usual came by automobile and the Canadian Pacific Railroad from Montreal or Nova Scotia. Roads all over the state had improved. With greater access to the fabled Maine wilderness, vacationers, hunters, fishermen, and outdoor enthusiasts came in ever increasing numbers.

The Game Warden Service grew as the tourists multiplied. One added mission of the Service was that of marine safety. The legislature had provided funds for them to purchase, equip, and administer several well-equipped motorized launches to fulfill the safety function. It also gave them greater efficiency in carrying out their primary function of fish and wildlife management and enforcement.

One incident at the northwestern part of Moosehead Lake took place that summer, involving Evan and his immediate superior, Captain Jim Melee. The two wardens were just leaving the headquarters building for lunch when a phone call interrupted them. Jim answered the phone. Evan could hear that the voice on the phone was hysterical. Jim listened carefully, his face turning white. Something bad had happened, Evan thought! Jim interrupted the caller, telling him that he and Evan were responding immediately and hung up.

Jim turned on his heel and bolted for the door. "C'mon, Evan, we've got a nasty hostage situation on our hands at Kineo. The sheriff needs help." They ran to the dock for one of the newly acquired launches with a six-cylinder Continental engine capable of pushing the craft up to fifty miles per hour. It was not unusual for the wardens to assist their law enforcement brothers; all of the wardens were trained and certified to act as police officers when none were available.

Jim handled the boat while Evan unlocked the equipment chest in the small forward cabin. He selected two Remington semi-automatic .35 caliber carbines, with shoulder slings, and two boxes of ammunition for each of them. They normally carried sufficient ammunition for their Colt .38 specials on their holster belt. He left the cabin and stood beside Jim at the helm, balancing himself on a rail handle.

Jim had a stern look about him. "About all I could understand from the caller was that a middle-age tourist went berserk over something his wife did to him. He started shooting up the reception area at the golf course near the foot of Kineo Mountain. They already have two dead bodies, they believe one of them is the man's wife. He's got a Savage .300 rifle and two hostages with him. They believe one is a small boy. The sheriff has him pinned down in an elevated location at the base of the mountain. Only two deputies are at the scene. I hope more help is forthcoming. Our first task is to cut off any escape route and to begin negotiating with the man, if we can."

Jim was, like Evan, an Army veteran, determined and cautious at the same time. Evan liked working with his superior whom he had come to love like a brother. They functioned well as a team, frequently reacting the same to situations that demanded life-and -death decisions.

It took them twenty minutes to arrive at the small bay in the shadow of the precipitous cliffs of Kineo. Several boats of curiosity-seekers had surrounded the area. They saw one of the deputies frantically motioning for them to beach the launch where he was standing. Jim did not hesitate to drive the launch part way onto the shore, cutting the engine. They both knew the deputy, Joe Hansen.

"What's the situation, Joe?" Jim asked, accepting the carbine Evan handed to him.

Deputy Hansen was worried. "As far as we know, he's still up there with a ten-year-old boy and a young waitress from the Inn. Those who witnessed what took place think she is injured. The killer tied the boy and girl together with a clothesline and pulled them across the golf course heading for the mountain. Deputy Hayes and I tried to make contact with him. His response was two shots fired in our direction from that small shelf with the two spruce trees leaning outward." Joe Hansen pointed to the exact location.

"Is he still there?" Jim asked.

"Yes, we heard the girl cry out to tell us she was all right. The man asked for a motorboat to safely leave the area. He said he'd leave the two hostages on the shore at Northeast Carry," Joe explained. "I think he's planning to head for Canada by foot. Do you have a megaphone in your launch, Jim?"

"Would you check, Evan?"

"I saw one in the locker when I picked up the rifles. I'll get it," Evan replied, leaping into the launch to pass the megaphone to Joe. "I've been thinking. The shooter is looking for a way out of here. He can't go any higher up the cliff with his two hostages. If you could make contact with him, Joe, offer him the chance to leave the area, provided the hostages are okay. Let's assume he's planning on reaching Canada. The nearest border is northwest of here where he could make it through the forest in two days or less."

"I agree with you so far, Evan. What do you suggest?" Jim asked, knowing that his partner had something definite in mind.

"He's already told you he'd release the hostages at Northeast Carry. That area is still wilderness. I'm sure that a private boat owner would agree to bring Jim and me to the area where we could wait for the man's arrival. I know the area well and suggest that we be dropped off at Seboomook Point where we can watch the Northeast Cove and the

Northwest Cove, which is ten miles closer to the Canadian border."

Jim thought about Evan's plan. "I like that alternative better than a direct assault on the shooter's current location."

"We'll need to carry a canoe with us," Evan also suggested. "We could hide it from view of the shooter, and use it once he has made landfall. We could quietly approach his landing location without him hearing anything. Then we could pick up his trail."

"The call is yours, Joe," Jim added, looking at the deputy. "Before we do anything we should make certain that the two hostages are alive."

Joe Hansen was a moderate man with a calm disposition. He liked Evan's proposal. "We'll give it a trial," he said, reaching for the megaphone. "Ahoy, you on the hillside. This is Deputy Hansen. I will agree to a motor launch made available to you, provided you can assure me that the two people you have with you are unharmed. Do you understand my terms?"

The man answered that they were still with him. Each of them screamed in hysterical voices that they were all right. Joe then advised the man to use the same route down that he used on the way up to his current location, warning him that they would hold their fire as long as things went as planned. Their main concern was the safety of the captives.

A small cabin cruiser belonging to the golf course came to pick up Jim and Evan who laid low below the gunwales until they had gotten out of sight, then they quickly commandeered a canoe and two paddles, pulling it onto the deck of the cruiser. The sleek and fast Chris-Craft headed for Seboomook at high speed. They were dropped off at Seboomook Point, with the canoe, where they had a clear view to the east and west with a pair of powerful binoculars.

An hour later, they picked up the sound of a screaming outboard motor. It had to be their man. Their instincts had been correct. The craft was heading for the most northern part of Moosehead Lake closest to the Canadian border. Jim studied the occupants from a safe place behind some fir saplings. He saw the two hostages sitting on the bottom of the boat.

Just as soon as the boat passed the inlet to the cove, Jim and Evan dragged the Old Town canoe into the water and began paddling. They had placed two small spruce trees in the front of the canoe to hide any outline of their bodies in case the shooter was checking his back trail. Evan knew that Joe and a posse would be in hot pursuit with their launch. The single hope for the culprit was a rapid flight to the Quebec boundary line. Ten minutes later, they pulled the canoe beside the beached boat. Jim pointed to a young lady sitting on the shore holding her head in her hands. They leaped out of the canoe, rushing to her side.

"How badly are you hurt?" Jim asked. "Where is the little boy?"

The woman looked into his eyes with a cry of relief. "The little boy is with the beast. The man's name is Jean Caron, a Canadian. The boy is his step-son. He hit me with his rifle." Her head was still bleeding.

"What is your name, young lady?" Evan asked in a calm voice.

"Caroline. I worked as a waitress at the dining room," she replied, still holding her head with her bloody hands.

Jim took a clean handkerchief from his pocket and wrapped it around her head. "Caroline, my partner and I have got to pursue Jean Caron before he harms the boy. You stay right here. Help is on its way. Do you understand?"

"Yes, I'll be fine. He's so angry with his wife he may kill the boy simply because of his mother. He wants to get to the border."

"We know, and we intend to prevent that. Be patient, Caroline. We'd like to stay with you, but the little boy needs our help more than you do."

"I understand, please hurry."

With that, Jim and Evan picked up the trail, unslinging their carbines to insert a round in the chamber. The trail was relatively easy to determine for trained observers like Evan and Jim. The heavy rains for the past few days made the ground soft, leaving distinct footprints. The moist forest floor allowed them to pursue the culprit quieter than usual.

A half hour into the pursuit Evan and Jim began climbing a steep incline when they heard a loud cry from the boy on the reverse of the slope as if he had been hurt. Jim, a father of two children, threw caution to the wind and leaped to the crest of the knoll, rifle at the ready. Evan was right behind him, his heart pounding.

The instant Jim looked down the reverse slope he was met by a bullet fired by Caron from a kneeling position, waiting for the pursuers to show themselves. Jim doubled over, dropping his rifle. Evan's first impulse was to stop the mad killer. He instinctively raised the Remington auto-loader to his shoulder, placing four shots into the killer's body. Then he kneeled to check Jim, frightened at what he would find. Jim was dead. A large opening at the back of his head was gushing blood onto the ground. There was a grotesque expression on his face as if to say, "Oh no, not now!"

Evan dropped his rifle to pick up Jim's lifeless body, rocking back and forth, screaming at the top of his lungs, "Why? Why Jim..."

The violent death of such a good man as Jim Melee enraged Evan to the point where he questioned his faith in a just God. He was no stranger to death on the battlefield, but that was different. The main objective was the death of their opponents. It was kill or be killed. He was consumed with despair. He wept for Jim and the two children who were so close to their father, and he wept for himself. Loud cries of agony parted his lips, piercing the deathly silence of the wilderness. How was he going to relay such a devastating message to Jim's wife and two children? The message was certain to tear three people's lives apart. He was unable to rationalize the death to himself, how could he give consolation to the family in their hour of greatest need?

Joe Hansen and several deputies arrived at the scene. He surveyed the situation, making sure that the dead man's son was being taken care of by two Greenville police officers. Turning to Evan and Jim with a shocked expression on his face, he kneeled down to embrace both of them. Over the years he had worked often with the dedicated slain warden, and was a part of his inner circle of close friends. Evan was still holding Jim covered with blood from his ugly wound.

"Come, Evan," Joe said in a quivering voice. "Let's take Jim home."

Evan opened his eyes, recognizing Joe. The depth of his pain was evident in his eyes. For a moment, Joe was frightened that Evan had slipped over the edge. He grasped Evan and held him. "He was my friend, too, Evan. You did all that could be done to back him up..."

"But I could have acted quicker... Why wasn't it me instead of a good man with a family?" Evan cried out in anguish, weeping openly in Joe's arms. After several minutes of convulsive sobs, he freed himself of Joe's support and gently placed Jim's body on the ground.

Without a word, Evan walked directly to Jean Caron's inert body silently standing over it. He turned to see the man's son softly crying in the arms of a Greenville policeman. "Okay, Joe. Let's take Jim back to Greenville."

The funeral for the fallen warden was attended by a large collection of wardens and police officers from several states. Even a group of Canadian Mounted Police were present to pay tribute to a fallen comrade. After the heart-wrenching funeral service and committal service, Evan stood over the closed casket for a final good-bye, filled with grief and anguish, and still questioning why...

Deputy Joe Hansen stood solemnly beside him, a witness to his pain. "Only time will tell, Evan. God never takes any of us home until we've completed our mission here on earth. Have faith, He knows what He's doing. It wasn't your time..."

Chapter Fourteen

Seven Years Later, October 29, 1929

Evan rushed home after a busy day in the field in the new Ford Model A pickup truck the state had provided the game warden service. It was a more practical vehicle for the wardens than an automobile. He was concerned for Joleen, his wife of seven years. It was their anniversary. Seven years of happiness and contentment. The gentle Joleen gave meaning to his life, especially after the trauma of losing his dear friend Jim Melee.

He was met at the door by their four-year-old daughter, Rena, a happy child with a mild disposition like her mother. Her long black hair was neatly done up in two braids with pink ribbons tied at the ends. Daddy's return each evening was a high point of her life. Evan swept her off her feet, holding her close to his heart. She was the joy of his life.

"I've been watching for you, Daddy."

"I rushed home as quickly as I could, Honey. Have you been a good girl for Mommy?" he asked, walking into the kitchen with her still in his arms.

Joleen met them with a smile. Two of the most important people in her life always made her smile. They had brought joy and definition to her life so completely that she was afraid it might not last forever. She embraced both of them. "Welcome home, Daddy. Rena is anxious to show you how well she colored some pictures in her coloring book. She also helped Mommy make a batch of peanut butter cookies."

Evan placed Rena on one of the chairs at the large table in the kitchen and turned to Joleen with a frown. "What's wrong, Evan?" she asked.

"Just before I left the headquarters, we received word from the commandant of our National Guard unit that we have been called up to reinforce the police in Augusta, Waterville, and Portland. The financial crisis has caused a lot of unrest. Billions of dollars have been lost in the stock market collapse. The runs on the banks are turning nasty. I hope that your accountant has been diligent and responsible with your investments."

"I heard about the crash on the radio. The accountant has not contacted us. Most of the inheritance went to purchase the two thousand acre tract at Little and Big Wilson Rivers. Possibly some will be lost, I just don't know," she told him, shaking her head, resigned to accept whatever the future would bring.

Shortly after they were wed, Joleen insisted in using some of the money to make improvements to the house that they would all enjoy. The proud Evan objected at first. He wanted to be able to provide for his family. She understood and agreed that she would think the same if she was in his position. From the very beginning of their relationship she had insisted that she too wanted to make a contribution, and that her inheritance was available for the common good. To ignore its potential to improve their lives would be misplaced pride.

They added a bathroom, a septic system, a new oil-fired furnace to supplement their wood stoves, and a complete remodeling of the kitchen. Evan was the first to agree that the improvements added to the quality of their lives together. Joleen's passion for buying land was satisfied with one more parcel adjoining the one owned by her sister in Kokadjo. The balance of the money was placed aside for future use for the children's education and any other family expenditure that came up. The money made them financially secure, and both Joleen and Evan agreed that the family was to continue the frugal type of life style that Evan had pursued before she entered the picture.

Evan turned to his wife and took her in his arms. She felt secure in his strong embrace. "My dear wife has been very generous and has made life a lot easier. I'm thankful for that, but more important than monetary things, I'm thankful for the ray of sunshine you've brought into our lives. Amie loves you and your soft ways. Harmony and contentment have been a part of my life since you agreed to marry me. I'm a lucky man." He kissed her gently as she laid her head against his chest. "I wish I did not have to leave, but the CO has activated our regiment. We're pulling out tonight. I'm taking one company to Augusta. Captain Knight is sick and unable to go with the company, so the Colonel gave me that responsibility even though I'm only a first lieutenant. I hope I'm good enough to handle the job."

She placed a finger to his lips. "Erase those doubts from your head, my husband. You'll do just fine. Be yourself, and the men will appreciate your concern and respond positively to your efforts."

Fortified with that kind of support, Evan quickly changed into his uniform and left for Greenville. The three companies drew full battle gear and supplies to sustain them in the field for a week. Buses of every description were hired to transport the regiment to their assigned destinations. It was too cold to transport them in the back of trucks for such long distances. Evan's company went to Augusta where they were needed to reinforce the regular police detachment of the city.

Primarily, the Guard units were used to cordon off and protect the State Capital and other government buildings and all of the banks in the city proper. Martial law was declared by the Governor. Large crowds had attacked some of the banks. The general mood was angry and restless, driven by fear of the unknown and the perceived image of economic disaster. The custodians of the peace were tested by several groups who physically attacked them with sticks and bare fists. Evan ordered each man to give ground and call for backup by his mobile reserve squad standing by in a truck, if they were threatened.

Eventually emotions were calmed, and the need for such tight security lessened. Two of Evan's platoons were released from duty and returned to Greenville four days after the deployment. Evan remained with his single platoon who still maintained a secure perimeter around the Capital Building. The presence of a guardsman with a bayonet attached to his rifle was a very effective deterrent to those attempting to gain access to the building. Twenty-four hours later they were on their way home, buoyed by the praise they received from the Governor.

Joleen frantically checked on their finances, discovering that they had lost thirty percent of her inheritance. She was surprised at her lack of concern for the loss. She had primarily valued the inheritance for what it represented, a generous token of her father's love and devotion for her. She knew better than anyone that it was nice to have a few luxuries in one's life, but it certainly did not purchase happiness or resolution to conflicts that arise in every family's lives.

She was proud to support Evan and to instill the values that had sustained the average American for generations. Hard work and frugality were the milestones of the working class of which Evan was proud to be a part. He never lost his respect for the common man and for his trials and tribulations.

Amie was a young lady when they were married. It took a while for both to get used to the situation, but mutual respect and affection soon developed into a warm friendship similar to that of two sisters. Evan had been a regular churchgoer before the war. Joleen suggested that they reinstate church attendance. She claimed she needed the strength her faith gave to her. They attended church regularly at the local Baptist Church.

That winter was the beginning of a long and severe depression which influenced the lives of every citizen in the country. Those who lived in the cities were hit more severely than their country brethren who could at least plant a garden and raise chickens and pigs to help feed their families. Many prosperous companies closed their doors permanently, leaving the work force in desperate straits to survive.

The two quarries closed down temporarily. There were no customers for their finely crafted slate products. Many families reverted to the old time system of bartering things they had or could make for goods or services from their neighbors. Stuff for stuff became a way of life which benefited most of the community. The elderly and physically limited folks suffered the most, but the churches in town worked diligently to generate assistance for those most in need. Hunger was not widespread, but it did exist.

Jobs of any description were just not available. Men would often line the road, soliciting work from passing motorists. Bob Gibson used to watch the road and ran out to intercept the local highway agent when he saw his truck. Occasionally the agent had enough money in his budget to give him a day or two of work on the roads. He was refused more than he could accept, leaving the majority dispirited and apprehensive about how they were going to get by. Fear and despair permeated the country. The depression was well-named. It created hardships and misery indiscriminately within society regardless of social standing.

Evan and Joleen made a point of living on his salary as a warden. Even that was limited. The state cut their budget in half. He worked only three days a week instead of six. He always enjoyed working in the woods. When his job was cut he went into the woodlands that were a part of the property and began cutting and processing firewood. The trusty and faithful work horse proved to be invaluable. He used the firewood to barter with those who had more tillable land, trading wood fuel for apples and potatoes. Bob and Joyce spent more time on their farm operations. Evan and Joleen traded wood for eggs, milk, and when they were ready for slaughter, half of a pig.

That October, Evan helped Bob butcher the four pigs he had raised. He took the bacon slabs, shoulders, and hams back home to place in a brown sugar and vinegar brine until they were ready for smoking in his smoke house. Evan's father had the most popular pickling brine formula in town. Evan had helped with the process every fall since he was a small child. The bacon and ham were sweet and tasty. He divulged the formula to no one, including Bob. The old smokehouse retained the aroma of smoked meats for months after the season ended.

To those families struggling on the edge of disaster, the winters in northern Maine were long and difficult. Starvation or at least hunger from not having enough to satisfy one's appetite lingered just around the corner. The spring of 1930 was notable for its severity. Many were at the breaking point. Usually spring is looked upon as the renewal of life, a time when life replenished itself. Normally it cultivated hope. That year it brought the populations to the stark reality that economic possibilities were getting scarcer than ever. Hard times were beginning to be a way of life. Tension and dread were the norm within most families. Job potentials were simply not available regardless of the price.

One day in late September 1930, Evan began his traditional patrol of the Little Wilson River watershed, walking the full length of the stream from its confluence with Big Wilson, on land Joleen had purchased, to its meager beginning near the town of Shirley Mills. He traveled westerly with the sun at his back during the early morning hours, and walked into the setting sun in the afternoon. The fourteen mile trek usually took two days. He checked licenses of any sportsmen he met along the way and made notes in his daily log of habitat conditions and signs and sightings of deer, bear, moose and partridge.

About four miles into his patrol, Evan planned to stay at a rustic log cabin built by several of his friends and neighbors in Monson. It was located on the south bank of the Little Wilson where the Appalachian Trail crossed the stream on its northerly azimuth toward Mount Katadin. The camp was frequently used by hikers, sportsmen, and managers of the Great Northern Paper Company's vast forest holdings who might seek its shelter. The builders of the cabin paid Great Northern one dollar per year for ninety-nine years.

The isolated cabin was equipped with a cast iron stove for heat and cooking; two wide bunks capable of sleeping six men; and a large table. Several assortments of chairs had been collected over the years. Bedding was rolled into a large bundle and suspended by thin wires in the middle of the cabin away from rodents. Those men who built it over a couple of years intended it to be a retreat where they could hunt and fish in an isolated environment. It turned out to be a retreat for troubled souls as much as a sportsmen's cabin in the Maine wilderness.

Whenever Evan stayed at the cabin, he replenished the dry firewood he had used during his stay. It was an old Maine custom that was rarely violated. Most left a note of their occupancy in a notebook suspended on a string with attached pencil near the door. There was a storage cellar behind the cabin about four feet deep for the storage of kerosene for lamps, candles, coffee, tea and anything else that was left over from a visit to the cabin. Normally there was a large assortment of canned foods stored there for emergency purposes.

Evan approached the cabin from a ridge on the north side of Little Wilson overlooking the cabin below. He had detected the smell of smoke for some distance, indicating the cabin was being used. Anxious to see who was present at the cabin, he slid down the ridge across the stream on a large white spruce tree that had been felled to bridge the rushing water. He noted that a small deer was hanging from a large yellow birch branch at the side of the cabin. A hind quarter had been removed from the deer carcass.

Uncertain who was inside, Evan checked that his .38 Colt revolver was loaded and ready for use. He removed his pack, holding it in his left hand, and knocked on the door. "Hello, inside."

"The door is unlocked, come on in," a voice answered him. Opening the door, Evan met Pierre Johnson, a neighbor on Tenney Hill. "We're surprised to see you, Evan," the tall muscular Swede greeted him with a warm handshake. Pierre was well-liked in the small rural community of Monson. Modest and gentle by nature, he was also one of the strongest men Evan had ever met.

"Well, I started on my Little Wilson patrol wondering if there would be room at the cabin," Evan replied, placing his pack inside the door.

The other two men, Hal Stanchfield and Raymond Leroux, welcomed him as one. Evan paused a few seconds to adjust to the darkness of the cabin. It was lit only by a kerosene lamp and a small candle on the long table opposite the stove. They were getting ready to eat supper. He was among friends he knew very well and was sincerely welcomed to stay the night and to share their food.

"We unanimously voted Pierre to be the cook while at camp," Ray told him with a good-natured chuckle. "He's a good cook but a might on the slow side."

"You're just in time, Evan," said Pierre, setting a tin plate on the table for him. "We've got venison steak, baked beans, and the best biscuits you ever tasted, thanks to my reflector oven. Grab one of those boxes for a seat. Some asshole burned two of our wooden chairs in the stove and left the cabin without a stick of wood. Times are changing..."

They sat around the table close to the kerosene lamp. "You're right, Pierre. These biscuits are sure better than Marie does at home on her new cook stove," Hal said, sitting next to Evan.

"I didn't expect this kind of treatment," Evan exclaimed. "Normally I run these patrols on a limited amount of food I have to carry. Several cans of sardines usually carries me through. I appreciate your hospitality, guys. This old cabin has seen many good times for all of us."

"We have some steaming hot water for tea, Evan. I prefer coffee, myself, but tea is easier to fix in the field," Hal offered, retrieving a teakettle from the stove.

"That's fine with me. Thanks, Hal."

The Maine woods cultivates healthy appetites. Meals are traditionally taken with a minimum of small talk. The four men consumed a dozen large biscuits, two pans of thinly sliced fried venison steaks, and a quart and a half of baked beans. The hearty meal satisfied each of them.

"Why is it that food tastes better out here in the woods than it does back at home?" Hal mused. "I'll volunteer to clean up the plates and utensils while you guys sit back to relax with your pipes."

All of the men but Pierre smoked a pipe. Evan passed around a pouch of Half and Half tobacco before filling his own corn cob pipe. Pierre finished his meal and took a pinch of snuff from a small round tin and placed it beneath his tongue. The only time he did not have a pinch in his mouth was at mealtime and when he was asleep. His skill at hitting a one pound coffee can with a spit of juice was legendary. "Well, Hal. I'm gonna let ye do the dishes. I don't want to get me hands all shriveled up like a prune," Pierre snickered with a mischievous grin.

That evening after supper Pierre placed his new 30-30 Winchester Model 94 carbine on the table to clean and oil. Ray did the same with a Savage.300 rifle he had borrowed from his brother-in-law. Hal challenged Evan to a game of cribbage at one cent a point to the winner.

The cribbage board was battered and scratched. Wooden matches served as pegs for the board. Both men took the game seriously as they puffed on their pipes, filling the cabin with smoke. Pierre grumbled that smoking was bad for their health and opened the door to air out the cabin. Everyone groaned in protest.

Pierre grinned with a twinkle in his eye. "Now, now, be patient boys. My eyes are burning. I don't know how you can see the cards you're playing." He held an empty coffee can at arm's length and spit directly in the opening. Proud of his accomplishment he closed the door with a smile.

Evan had the same warm feeling of camaraderie that he had experienced in the Army in France. He lost three games to Hal, owing him eighteen cents. They retired early. Hal and Evan took the top bunk and soon fell sound asleep. The soft whir of the wind through the fir and spruce trees beside the cabin blended with the bubbling of the water flowing over a rocky river bed was like music to their ears.

The first to rise was Pierre who started the fire and prepared the same meal they had for supper – beans, steaks and biscuits with hot tea. There was a little less friendly banter in the morning. Breakfast was consumed perhaps quicker than their supper. Each had their day planned and were preparing for it.

Evan told them he had to push on right after breakfast so that he could make it to Shirley by nightfall. "Thanks for your hospitality, guys. I've enjoyed my stay, as always."

There was an air of apprehension in the cabin as he was dressing to leave. He pulled on his pack and approached the door, turning to face his friends.

"It is my belief that many natural laws of survival preceded the State of Maine game laws. I also understand that these hard times require adaptation. Now, I have no objection for you guys to pack out as much meat to feed your families as you can carry. Being responsible for a family is something that each of you take seriously, and I admire your steadfastness. However, I must tell you that if any of you try to sell the meat downtown, it's all over. Please, I ask you as a friend, don't make me enforce that rule. Give my best to your wives and kids when you get home. Again, thanks for a pleasant stay."

With that, Evan walked out the door to continue his patrol.

Chapter Fifteen

Joleen had been reviewing the progress of a building project that had been dear to her father's heart. It was a public library for the very small town of Moody, West Virginia, located in the north central portion of the Appalachian Mountains. Before Lamont Carpenter passed away, he made certain that a grant he was leaving the community would be sufficient to construct the building and to stock its shelves with several thousand volumes. Joleen's mother had been instrumental in insuring that his wishes were carried out.

The project sounded like an interesting one to Evan who shared their enthusiasm. He questioned members of the family about its progress whenever they came to Maine for weekend retreats or vacations. He was looking forward to attending, along with his family, the commissioning ceremony and opening of the library to the general public, scheduled for the second week in October. At the last minute Rena came down with a bad cold. Evan and Joleen agreed it would not have been prudent to take the child on such a lengthy trip in October. Evan suggested that he stay at home with Rena while Joleen went to the event. She had been looking forward to showing off her husband and daughter to the extended group of family and friends that would be present. She reluctantly gave in to his suggestion, disappointed that she would be traveling alone.

Evan drove her to Newport where she could catch a train for Boston with easy connections for the rest of the country. Rena stayed with Bob and Joyce for the day. At the last minute Joleen was hesitant to leave. Evan dismissed her concern with a warm embrace. "I'll be with you in spirit all the time. You're very beautiful in your dark green dress, my love. I'll miss you, but I want you to be with your family to share this occasion in memory of your very generous father. He would be proud

117

that his creation has brought his family together again, sharing the fulfillment of his dream."

"That's all the more reason I so wanted to have you and Rena at my side," she exclaimed.

He kissed her two eyes. "Now go, Joleen. The train is waiting. I'll meet you here when you return. I love you and will miss you."

She clung to him, returning his kiss. "I love you, too. I'll miss my very special family. Don't forget to have Rena brush her teeth. You'll have to watch her closely on that. She claims the toothpaste is too salty," she smiled at him.

"I won't let her get away with anything, Mother," he replied, placing her suitcase on the train transom.

She took a seat next to a window where he could see her. She waved until the train pulled out of sight. Evan felt an instant loneliness creep over him. It was the first time they had been away from each other since they were married. From that very special moment, he was filled with contentment. She had a unique way of soothing his worries with a warm embrace or an encouraging word. He was not complete without her at his side.

While he was in Newport, he had their Model A Ford sedan greased and the oil changed where they had purchased it. Bob was outside throwing firewood into his shed when Evan pulled into their driveway. "Hi, Evan. You're just in time to sample some of Joyce's baked beans and fresh boulla rolls she should be taking out of the oven about now. You didn't eat, did you?"

Evan returned his smile. "How can a hungry man refuse that invitation? I see that you've got most of your wood supply bucked up and piled."

"Yeah, it's always a struggle to get it under cover before snowfall."

Evan followed Bob into the kitchen where Rena was already sitting at the table. "Rena has been a lot of help to Aunt Joyce. We folded clothes and baked some peanut butter cookies, then she had a good long nap. She's kind of uncomfortable with her cold, but she'll survive."

The radio in the living room was on and just as they sat down to the table, Roberta's latest recording of *When The Moon Comes Over the Mountain* began to play. Everyone at the table listened carefully to her rich soprano voice filling the airwaves. The years that had passed since their parting had softened Evan's hatred towards her. Joleen had helped him overcome the hurt. Reliving the past was counter-productive to happiness. Roberta's rendition of the very popular song was flawless. He wished her well, for she still had that indefinable ability to give a good song a soul that touched her audiences. Her selection of songs were in keeping with her small-town rural American legacy.

Joyce got up to turn off the radio when the recording stopped. She was the first to speak. "She still has that touch we all experienced in Monson."

"I think that is one of her best," Evan added quietly, anxious to change the subject. "Bob, you mentioned that you wanted to turn more of your woodland into field land so that you could raise more corn and other truck crops. I've been considering something along that same line. Perhaps you and I can join hands to clear that old cut-over parcel of four or five acres in my southeast corner against your western boundary. The soil there is richer and more rock-free than any other section we own. We could harvest the pole-size hardwood sprouts for firewood. What do you think?"

Bob had followed his words with interest. "If we cut the stuff leaving high stumps, they could be removed with a good team of draft horses. I like the idea, Evan. A good bog harrow would smooth out the area after the stumps are removed, making an ideal seedbed for new crops. What do you suggest we do to make it fair?"

"You and I can harvest the firewood on those days I'm off. We can go fifty-fifty on the wood," Evan suggested.

Bob thought about the proposition. "You're very generous with your offer, Evan. No one knows how long this depression and loss of jobs will last. Those of us lucky enough to live in the country can at least raise our own food. Even if we don't have time to clear all of the parcel you have in mind, we could use it for pasture for beef cows for a year or so, or maybe pigs. If I do that I'll go fifty-fifty with you on whatever the land produces, whether it's vegetables or meat."

"Then it's a deal, Bob," Evan reached over the table to shake his friend's hand. "I still work three days a week, mostly every other day. I don't mind getting an early start on the firewood before heavy snows make it a lot harder."

He was just finishing his second boulla roll. "My, my, Joyce, your rolls are the best in town. I speak as an authority who has sampled most of the folk's efforts over the years."

Joyce blushed. "Thank you, Evan."

Rena left the table to lie down on the couch in the living room. Joyce placed a blanket over her. "She's sleeping a lot. That's the best thing for her."

"It's not nice to eat and run, but I should take her home. The house will be getting cold. Thanks for a great supper, Joyce, and thanks for taking care of Rena. What do you say if we get to the clearing job as soon as possible, Bob? You can keep my Belgian in your barn; that way you'll have the team in one place."

"You bet, Evan. Thanks for being so generous."

Joyce wrapped Rena in a second blanket for her trip in the car. "She's such a precious child. She talks and acts like a much more mature little girl. You two have done a wonderful job with her." She leaned over to whisper in his ear, "I plan to tell Bob tonight that I'm pregnant." She was flushed with happiness.

"God bless you, Joyce. Bob's a lucky man," he whispered back to her.

Evan rushed home to put Rena in her bed so that she would not be cold. He was banking the stoves for the evening when the phone rang. It was Joleen. "Hello, Evan, I didn't realize it was so late."

"Are you okay, Honey?" Evan anxiously asked.

"I'm fine, just missing my husband, that's all. How is Rena tonight?"

"She's sound asleep. Her cold is not getting any worse. She ate well at Bob's and Joyce's tonight. When are you coming home, Joleen?"

"That's mainly what I'm calling about. Several of Father's friends are working on plans to help relieve the massive unemployment of younger men in the work force. There's talk of an effort to enroll unemployed men to carry out conservation projects such as building access and fire roads, fire towers, and timber stand improvement measures in our forestlands. Have you heard anything about such a program?"

Evan told her that he had several directives on his desk in Greenville suggesting a list of useful projects that might be included in such a vast conservation program to be administered by the Army or National Guard units. She sounded enthusiastic about the potential of such programs.

"Why the sudden interest, Honey?"

"I've been thinking about our Elliotsville tract of land. What are your thoughts if I was to turn it over to the state to administer as a state park?"

It was the first time she had mentioned such a possibility. "If that's what you want to do, Honey, then I support your generous proposal. It is a lovely area that could be enjoyed by a greater number of people if it was suitably accessible for visitors. If that is the reason for your excitement, of course I agree with your efforts and will help wherever I can. I love you, Joleen."

"Oh, Evan. Thank you for agreeing with me. I'll be home day after tomorrow on the noon train at Newport. We can talk more specifically about the subject when I'm home. I love you and miss you, too. Until next time."

"We'll be at the station when your train pulls in."

That evening Evan reviewed their conversation. When she purchased the parcel of land with a portion of her inheritance from her father, he insisted that she keep it separate from their family finances.

He wondered how his National Guard unit might be used in administering such a program as Joleen described. The next morning he dropped off Rena with his Aunt Mildred and drove to Greenville where he inquired with his base of operations in Augusta. He was told that the Maine Game Warden Service and Forest Service would assume advisory positions for a proposed Civilian Conservation Corp made up of unemployed men. He was surprised that he had not been more informed.

Most of that morning he made out a list of possible "make-work" projects in his region. Hiking trails, fire towers, roads, and camping sites were always useful construction projects, but most of the land north of Moosehead was owned by the Great Northern Paper Company. He had no authority to interfere within their domain. The state was responsible for the game population on private land. As a game warden, Evan

121

was most conscious of the constitutional rights of private ownership of land. He always carried out his duties in a spirit of cooperation with the land owners. Their rights superseded the regulations of the State of Maine, and he vigorously supported that basic law of the land.

A vast government sponsored program was about to be launched across the country. He could see some advantages of such an approach, but overall, he questioned the cost/benefit ratio normally used as a guiding factor in everything the Game Warden Service did. He was unabashedly concerned about so much government control of people's lives. Government bureaucracies were notoriously inefficient and wasteful of taxpayers' money.

He was unprepared to offer different solutions; yet, most hard-working citizens would use their initiative to solve their own problems. Large government handouts could cultivate a new wave of dependency on welfare. Politicians had a way of looking out for themselves. They basked in their own power to control those who allowed it to happen. Power was more dangerous than greed. A growing distaste of what was taking place bothered him all the way back home. His forefathers had a lot less when they settled in the wilds of Maine in the early 1700's. They did not look to the largess of the government. Their resourcefulness helped build the nation, carving a home and a way of life from the primitive land. The simple arrangement he and Bob had agreed on was a prime example of man solving his own problems.

Rena's cold was better the next morning, so Evan decided to take her with him to pick up Joleen. They were a little earlier than the train's estimated time of arrival and stopped at a small café next to the station to have a cup of hot cocoa. They took a seat so that he could see the station. Several people were huddled around a radio near the door to the kitchen. He could not hear what was taking place.

"What's on the radio?" Evan asked the waitress.

"You haven't heard the news?" she asked.

"No, we just drove from Monson."

"Well, there's been a train derailment near Boston. Several people have been killed.

Evan picked up Rena and ran to the station office. The person in charge didn't have any more information than what was on the radio. Evidently there were several people injured and a few dead. The station master told him that it could be hours before any more information was available. All rail lines were blocked for now. He might as well go back home and stand by a phone for specific information about his wife. Officials at the scene of the accident needed time to attend to those in need. He understood that aspect of the accident, but he was almost out of his mind with worry. He left his name and telephone number with the station master and carried Rena back to their Ford.

That trip home was the longest ride of his life. He was like a zombie, completely indifferent to everything around him. He could not erase the ugly images that consumed him. His Joleen had to be among the living. They had too much life ahead of them... How could he possibly exist without her??? How??? He screamed though no sound passed his lips.

As soon as he turned onto his street he saw deputy Joe Hansen's automobile in his drive. He prayed that Joe was the bearer of good news! He was standing on his porch with Bob and Joyce when Evan turned off the Ford and ran toward them.

"Joleen's okay, isn't she?" he cried. "She's all right..." Then he saw the sadness on Bob's face. Joyce was openly weeping.

Joe embraced Evan, holding him firmly. "You've got to be strong, Evan. I don't know any other way to say it... Joleen was killed in the crash!"

Chapter Sixteen

An inhuman cry pierced Evan's lips, and he collapsed in Joe's arms. His world was turned upside down. Bob reached out to take Evan in his arms, holding him like a baby. Joyce ran to the car to get Rena who was screaming out of control.

"Why is Daddy angry?" Rena asked Joyce.

"Your Daddy is not angry, Honey. Come, let me take you into the house. Your Daddy needs you more than ever now."

As soon as Joe had turned into the driveway, Bob and Joyce came running to him. They had heard the news about the train crash on the radio. Bob instantly went about getting the fires in the kitchen and parlor stoves going. It was going to be a long, cold night for Evan's family. How he dreaded the devastation his best friend was about to experience.

Joyce had contacted Amie working as a nurse at a Bangor hospital. She had finished her training two years before. The news crushed her. Amie had quickly taken Joleen into her heart when she married Evan. Joleen was the sister she never had. She told Joyce between sobs that she would be there on the next Hasey Maine Stage bus she could get, or maybe someone would drive her home. Brother and sister needed each other!

Joyce took Rena into her room to change her into a warm set of pajamas and a heavy bathrobe. She knew that Rena liked oatmeal and took her to the kitchen to prepare a warm meal for her. She also put on a pot of coffee for the adults.

Bob placed Evan on the couch in the living room off the kitchen. He was still unconscious. The pain of acknowledging his precious wife's death was just too much to accept. Bob covered him with a warm blanket and soberly walked into the kitchen.

124

"Joyce and I will stay with them tonight, Joe. I never dreamed we'd have to go through such an ordeal. He was devoted to her," Bob sighed.

Joe nodded in agreement. "I knew that. He's got a rough mountain to climb. Thank God he's got you two for neighbors. Where is Amie anyway?"

"I called her. She's a nurse at a Bangor hospital. She'll be on the next bus to Greenville."

"If you two need anything, please call me. He's my friend, too. You have my number. I'll stop by in the morning. May God help us." With that, Joe left the house.

Evan awoke from his emotional meltdown and looked around him. He sat up on the couch, holding his head in both hands. Bob, sitting in a chair opposite him, saw Evan sit up. Soon his body was wracked with convulsive shrieks. Bob went to place a comforting arm around his friend, feeling helpless.

"Can I fix you a hot cup of coffee or tea, Evan?"

"Yes," Evan replied in a hoarse voice. That was a positive answer!

Suddenly, an automobile turned into the driveway. Seconds later, Amie burst into the house. Seeing her brother sitting on the couch, she ran to hold him with tears streaming down her cheeks. "My dear brother. I got here as quickly as I could. What a terrible thing to have to go through." The driver of the automobile, a nurse friend, put Amies's suitcase in the living room and left them alone.

Bob set out a cup of coffee for Amie, glad that she could come so soon. She would be good for her brother. They sat most of the evening at the kitchen table talking, crying, and remembering those moments they had shared with Joleen. The day that Joleen moved into their house, their lives became more meaningful. She had a gift for bringing out the best in people. Peace and love radiated from her, touching everyone that stood within her aura.

That evening Evan told Bob, Joyce, and Amie that he wanted a funeral in their church in Monson. He informed them of her wish for the piece of land in Elliotsville, and his plan to have her buried there. All the next day Evan kept busy contacting Joleen's family, his superiors in Augusta, and several hours with his pastor in Monson. Amie took over the chores of the house, keeping a supply of coffee on the kitchen stove.

The funeral service was delayed for two days until the funeral director received Joleen's body. Waiting for that to take place was the cruelest and most hurtful period of all. Evan had received so many phone calls and visits from friends and acquaintances who wanted to wish him well and to convey their sympathy for his tragic loss. He was touched by the outpouring of support, but he silently screamed for everybody to just leave him alone so that he could mourn his beloved wife in solitude. Idle chatter was becoming mentally exhausting. The day of the funeral, he was just a shell of the man he used to be. He was living in a world like a robot, slightly out of touch with what was going on around him. Grief had overwhelmed him.

Several hundred people crowded into the small Baptist church. Ten of Evan's game warden friends acted as ushers in their colorful uniforms with red jackets. Evan wore a dark blue suit and matching overcoat. Rena sat between him and Amie. Bob and Joyce took seats immediately behind them in case they were needed. Joleen's mother and sister Aline sat on Evan's left in the front row. Both wore black dresses with black veils that hid the despair of losing one of their own on the very threshold of life. Evan was completely unable to comfort them. Joleen's violent death had triggered more pain and hopelessness than most of them were able to cope with.

Pastor Holt began the service with a hymn universally cherished by generations. Evan remained during the ceremony with his eyes fixated on the casket in front of him. Images of his short life with the gentle Joleen passed through his mind, fueling the pain that existed. When tears welled in his eyes, little Rena kissed him on the cheek and whispered, "Don't cry, Daddy, don't cry..."

When Pastor Holt had completed the short funeral service, he announced that they would immediately travel to the place of burial for a short interment. The game warden pallbearers solemnly carried the casket from the church to the waiting hearse for Joleen's final journey on this earth. Evan, Bob, and several close friends had worked tirelessly to prepare a proper burial location for Joleen on the knoll overlooking the spot where the Little Wilson and the Big Wilson Rivers met in a deep rock-strewn chasm of churning water and foam.

The funeral director had provided a limousine for the immediate family use. Joleen's mother and sister shared the back seat with Evan. Alex, Amie, and Rena sat on the small jump seats for the ride out to the burial site.

"The location you selected for Joleen is a beautiful one, Evan," Mrs. Carpenter sadly stated. "She loved the land more than any other place. It's most appropriate that you follow her wish to donate the land to the state for a park."

He squeezed her hand, replying in a strained voice, "I'm glad you approve…"

A raw wind blew across the grave site as the pallbearers placed the casket beside the open grave. The pastor briefly reviewed the short relationship he had experienced with Joleen. The simple statement of devotion brought Evan to tears again.

"Joleen has physically left our circle of friends and family. Yet, her remarkable spirit of selflessness and unfettered love are a lasting legacy that will always inspire those who were fortunate enough to know this very special lady. She now resides with the Lord, but her spirit will also be a daily part of the lives of her family which she dearly cherished. Good-bye, dear Joleen. Soon we, too, will make the same journey, and our reunion will be rejoiced. Amen."

The casket was slowly lowered by the wardens, and the long line of well-wishers passed the open grave to bid her a last farewell. Evan embraced Mrs. Carpenter and Alice, telling them to return to the village in the limousine. He wanted to be alone for a while with his wife. They understood and left the scene. Joyce and Bob told Evan that they were taking Amie and Rena back with them. Bob had driven Evan's Ford over the newly constructed roadway to the grave site and parked it for his use.

Evan spent an hour kneeling beside the grave, communing with his dead wife. He gave thanks for the privilege of sharing the precious time they had spent together, and prayed for the strength to be a worthy father for the child that was a product of their love for each other. Without her soft and reassuring touch, he was frightened and afraid of the journey that he had to face alone. Tears flowed down his cheeks until there were no more tears to be shed. He said good-bye to his gentle partner, promising to return to the lonely grave to share the events he and Rena experienced.

Unbeknown to Evan, a lone figure in a long black coat parked a vehicle at the entrance to the grave and slowly walked toward Evan, hesitant to intrude upon his private moments with the deceased. The cold wind swept across the landscape, an omen of the long winter months ahead. The figure stood silently beside him, flushed with sadness.

The person kneeled beside Evan and placed a comforting hand on his shoulder. "I'm so sorry for your loss, Evan."

Blinded with grief, he recognized that voice. It was Roberta!

"I came as quickly as I could make connections on the trains. I wanted you to know that old friends share your tragic loss."

He was speechless for a moment and was unwilling for Roberta to see him so vulnerable and helpless. "It's nice that you came. Old friends are important. If you had known her, you'd have loved her too."

"I'm sure that's true. I just met Bob and Joyce on their way home with Amie and Rena. I feel helpless here beside you because I know that nothing I or anyone else can say will ease the pain that's consuming you right now. Sometimes all one can do is to be present and to share a friend's sorrow and pain. You're not alone, old friend."

"Joleen helped me to push the anger I harbored for you out of my system. She filled me with so much love and peace and harmony that I could never find the words to describe how completely I loved her."

"I love your Joleen for helping you that way. I've carried a lot of regrets and self-loathing over the years. I'm so sorry for the pain I inflicted on you. I pray God will forgive me."

With that, Roberta kissed him softly on the cheek and left him alone at the grave.

Chapter Seventeen

Ten Years Later (Spring, 1940)

Evan turned his state vehicle into the headquarters building at Greenville. He had just left the state armory where he had officially been commissioned a first lieutenant in the Maine National Guard as executive officer of an infantry company. It was a position he had temporarily filled over the years. Today's promotion made it official. He had worked hard to serve the company and was pleased that his efforts had been rewarded.

There was a wistful look on his face as he entered his office. Amie and Rena were proud of him, but something was missing! Ten years ago all of his hopes and dreams for the future were burned to ashes when he buried his wife, Joleen. The hurt never left him. Everyone that knew Evan had seen a change in him. He rarely smiled or joked and went out of his way to avoid people, which was a distinct reversal of his disposition.

Six years ago he was promoted to the rank of captain in the warden service and took command of the regional office in Greenville with four wardens to assist him in the assigned area. He checked on the pilot of the plane stationed at the Greenville regional office who had just returned from a flight into the Allagash Region conducting moose and deer population counts.

At midday, he left for Monson to pick up a lunch at home before he continued to a meeting at a sportsman's club in Abbot. He picked up his mail at the Monson Post Office where he met an old classmate, Max Holland.

"Hi, Evan," Max greeted him with an excited look. Normally Max was a little shy and stuttered slightly. "Have you heard anything more about the killings?"

129

"What are you talking about, Max?"

"The rumor is that someone shot Pat and Henry Mackie, the two old hermits living in a cabin out on the Greenville road."

"I know the men you mention, Max." Thinking that he might be able to help, he leaped into his vehicle. "Thanks, Max. I'll see you around."

He turned up the road toward Greenville and into a rough driveway leading to the small camp the Mackie brothers lived in. They were two elderly recluses that never bothered anyone, keeping to themselves. He spotted Joe Hansen studying the smoldering remains of the cabin. Joe turned to see Evan getting out of his vehicle.

"I'm glad to see you, Evan. We may need you guys on this one," Joe told him. Evidently someone shot both men and burned the camp to hide what took place.

"Do you have any idea who might have done it?"

Joe went to his Ford to open the trunk. "We haven't questioned many people yet. We did find a rifle in the spruce thicket beside the camp." Joe pointed to the firearm.

Evan examined it carefully without touching it. "Most hunters are particular about their weapons. They become a personal item a lot like a toothbrush." Evan's experienced eye noted that it was a relatively new Winchester Model 94 .30-30 caliber rifle with a nickel receiver and a two-thirds magazine.

He instantly recalled that Pierre Johnson had a rifle just like it. "I'm pretty sure this is the same rifle that Pierre Johnson purchased from the hardware store in town a few years ago. We can confirm that by speaking to Pierre or to Mr. Pullen at the hardware store."

"Who's this Johnson fellow anyway?" Joe asked with interest.

"If you're thinking that it could be Pierre, get that thought out of your head, Joe. I know the man. He's living in the Pennington house down by the quarry. He's not your man, but he might know who is."

"Would you like to check that out for me, Evan? I've got to get the two corpses ready for transport."

"Sure, I'll head down there now."

Pierre and his family had lived for years on Tenney Hill, a short distance from Evan's place. He knew the family well.

Pierre had been ill for some time. Evan knocked on the door, hoping he was not disturbing Pierre's rest. His oldest son, Pete, answered the door. "Hi, Mr. Mundy."

"Hello, Pete. Is your dad able to answer a few questions right now?"

"Is something wrong?"

Evan told him the reason for his visit.

"Dad is still resting. I can tell you that Marshal Lovejoy borrowed Dad's rifle with a box of shells last week. He was thinking of purchasing the gun and wanted to try it out, so Dad let him take it. I was the one to hand the gun to Marshal. Woe! Do you think he shot those two old guys?" Pete exclaimed.

"It's a possibility. Give my best to your dad. I'll be in touch. Thanks, Pete."

"You're welcome, Mr. Mundy."

By the time Evan returned to the scene of the crime, a state policeman had taken over the investigation. Evan told him about Marshal Lovejoy. The policeman was interested.

"While I was on my way to Monson, I got a call from a trooper in Rockwood who had just stopped a Chevrolet coupe for speeding. The driver's name was Marshal Lovejoy."

"He's heading for the Canadian border," Evan exclaimed. "You better get on your radio to stop him, before he gets to the crossing, which is not too far away."

The trooper ran to his Ford to make the call. Evan walked around the smoldering ruins. There was a sweet smelling aroma in the air that made him gag. He'd experienced that same scent in France during the war. It was the smell of death.

The trooper called to him. "One of my men just reported that a Chevrolet coupe of the same description was abandoned on a logging road that crossed the Moose River."

Picturing the situation in his mind, Evan quickly replied: "I'll bet he's trying to make the border through the forest, probably heading for Boundary Bald Mountain area. We have some time before darkness settles in. It might be a good idea to take a look at that area from the air. We have a float plane tied up at our dock. It's your call, Trooper. What do you suggest?"

"By all means, Captain. If you wardens can cover the interior portions of the area, I'll saturate the roadways with troopers. We now have a good description of the man we're looking for."

"We'll do our best," Evan replied. "When I get to Greenville, I'll send one of our radio cars tuned to your frequency to the area."

Twenty minutes later, Evan was airborne with the plane heading for Rockwood twenty miles away. They followed along the Canadian Pacific railroad tracks to Moose River. A train just passed through the area. He ordered the pilot to radio ground patrols to stop and search that train, just in case their man was aboard. The pilot continued along the road to Jackman until they spotted the abandoned coupe surrounded by police vehicles.

From that point of reference, Evan instructed the pilot to drop as low as he was comfortable, and to fly a straight line to Boundary Bald Mountain to the northwest. They made several sweeps along the grid at about five hundred foot intervals, watching the ground for anything unusual. Suddenly they both spotted a figure dart through an opening in the forest canopy where pulpwood had recently been cut. The figure tried to hide behind a stump as they continued without deviation from their grid search routine.

There were remnants of a logging hut on a small pond two miles from the location where they spotted the man. Evan asked the pilot to drop down and let him out as near the cabin as he could safely maneuver, and to return to his assigned flights on the grid as if they had not seen the lone figure, and as quietly as possible. The pilot was an experienced flier who did as he was instructed. Evan was hoping that the man was heading for the cabin. He jumped out of the plane with a flare gun and waved the pilot off.

His plan was to wait near the cabin out of sight, praying that his instincts were correct. Selecting a secluded spot underneath a clump of pole-size spruce trees, he broke off two branches to better cover his body outline from inquiring eyes from the cabin, about two hundred feet away. The plane continued on its assigned flight path, hoping that his ploy would work. He had second thoughts that he would look foolish if the figure turned out to not be Lovejoy. He simply dismissed the possibility, hunched his shoulders, and slowly scanned the area around the cabin.

A half hour later, a moving sapling caught his attention. The air was too still to whip a tree of that size. Maybe it was a deer or a moose that had brushed the tree. He was not sure until a man stepped into plain view and stopped to look around him. Evan held his breath. It was Marshal Lovejoy! He had seen the man around town. He had moved into Monson a few years ago. One of his daughters was in Rena's class in school. Seeing no evidence of a weapon, Evan thought it would be easier to arrest him after he had entered the cabin.

Lovejoy approached the cabin with caution, stopping every few feet to look and listen. The old door was half open, wedged against the sill. He entered the cabin, probably ready to stay the night within its shelter. Evan waited ten minutes before he rushed the cabin with revolver drawn. He smashed the fragile door and leaped inside. Lovejoy was startled to see a warden holding a revolver on him.

"Lie down on the floor on your stomach, Marshal. I've been waiting for you. Place your two hands on the small of your back, now!"

Marshal did as he was ordered. There was a haggard look about him. His clothes were torn and wet. "I arrest you for the murder of the two Mackie brothers."

Marshal seemed resigned to his fate. Evan clasped his hands with a pair of cuffs. "Why, Marshal? Those two men were completely harmless and never bothered anyone. Why?"

"Someone told me they had some gold in the cabin. I never wanted it to turn out this way…," he buried his face into the soil floor of the cabin and wept.

"Your daughter is in the same class as mine. Didn't you think of her?" Evan asked, lifting him off the floor and pushing him outside the cabin. He never answered the questions. He simply stared at the ground, a beaten human being.

Evan saw the float plane turning towards the cabin and fired the flare gun as a signal for him to land. Five minutes later, Lovejoy was secured in the compartment area behind the two seats. "Let's head for Greenville," Evan called out to the pilot.

Two state policemen and Joe Hansen were waiting for them at the landing. Lovejoy was hysterical but cooperative as he was being taken away by the police.

"You did a great job of nabbing him, Evan," said Joe Hansen, filling his corn cob pipe. "You should have taken another man with you."

Evan shrugged his shoulders. "The important thing, Joe, is we've got him in custody now. I think I'll head home. Rena has been with Joyce and Bob since she got out of school."

"How old is your daughter, Evan?"

"She's a senior in high school come fall. I think she wants to be a nurse like my sister, Amie. I'd like that, too."

"My nephew is in your company at the National Guard. He has nothing but praise for your work with the infantry company."

Evan smiled. "I learned the hard way in France that training has to be thorough. It saves lives in combat. The way things look in Asia and Europe, we may become involved in some way. I hope not, but we must prepare for that contingency. We already have Navy and Coast Guard vessels escorting British ships across the Atlantic. It doesn't look good, Joe."

"You're right. I'm too old for service. I saw enough in the last war. Well, it's time to call it a day. Thanks for a job well done, Evan."

"I'll see you around, Joe."

The ride to Monson gave Evan a chance to review events of the day. He took no pleasure in arresting Marshal Lovejoy. All he could think of was the devastation taking place in the family. The girl in Rena's class was a shy quiet girl. The trauma of her father's actions would probably burden her for the rest of her life. Evan felt compelled to inform the family about his actions and was anxious to lend a helping hand if it was needed. He turned down Depot Street across the railroad tracks to the house where they lived. The name of the girl in Rena's class was Mena, Evan recalled. He was uncertain how many other children were in the family.

He knocked on the door. Mena opened it. "Hello, Mena. I stopped by to see if you or your mother needed anything."

Her eyes were red and her hair unkempt. She had the saddest look on her face he had ever seen on a human being. "The police came to tell us what happened. Are you the one who arrested him?"

Suddenly he felt guilty. "I did what had to be done, Mena. Is your mother at home?"

"She's lying down. She's not well. The news of what my father did has shamed us..." She turned away from him and cried holding her head in her two hands.

He stepped into the house to close the door and embraced her. He saw a small boy of four or five years sitting at the kitchen table eating a bowl of corn flakes. "Don't be frightened, son. Your sister will be okay. Where's your mother?"

The boy pointed to a room off the kitchen. Evan sat Mena down at a chair beside her brother and walked into the room. A lone figure was lying on a cot bundled in blankets.

"Mrs. Lovejoy, I'm Evan Mundy. Do you need a doctor?" he asked, looking closer so that he could see her face. The room was dark. She did not respond. He placed a hand on her forehead. She was running a slight fever. "Mrs. Lovejoy, can you hear me?"

She answered in a weak voice, "I hear you. Are you the one who arrested Marshal?"

"Yes. What can I do for you?"

She began to cry. "I hope this is all just a nightmare and I'll wake up to find that he did not kill those two poor men." She was becoming hysterical.

Evan never felt so helpless in his life. He turned to see Mena standing beside him. "What's wrong with your mother, child?"

"She's been very weak for several days. She and my father had a terrible fight. He slapped her hard in the face and left the house early this morning."

Evan returned to the kitchen with Mena. "When was the last time you had a meal? Tell me the truth, Mena?"

"We have some cereal...that's about it," she replied.

"Your mother needs a doctor. I'm leaving to get one. Do you have a phone?"

"No."

"Okay," he said, sickened by the family's desperate situation. "I'll be back shortly. You be a brave girl for your mother and brother. I'm going for a doctor and some food."

Mena began to cry again. He held her close in his arms. "Be strong, young lady."

135

He left the house angry that a husband and a father could leave his family in such desperate condition. He stopped to see Pastor Holt and Doctor Kerr. The family needed both professionals immediately. He quickly checked to see how much cash he had in his wallet and rushed to Cad Brown's store where he purchased bread, peanut butter, jelly, eggs, tea, milk, a brick of cheddar cheese, a piece of beef to make stew and an assortment of canned soups, vegetables, and fruits.

Pastor Holt was already at the Lovejoy home by the time he arrived there. Mena saw him on the porch with two bags of groceries and opened the door for him. Reverend Holt was in the bedroom with Mrs. Lovejoy.

"You can sort out these groceries, Mena. The doctor will be calling shortly. I'm going to leave now, but you've got to promise me something," he said to her.

Her eyes lit up when she saw what he had purchased for them. "Oh thank you, Mr. Mundy, I'll promise you anything."

"I want you to call me if there is anything you or your mother need. Can you promise me that?"

"You are a very kind man, Mr. Mundy. Yes, I will do that. Rena is lucky to have you for a father."

He quickly embraced her and left to pick up Rena at Joyce's and Bob's house.

Chapter Eighteen

The summer of 1940 was a time of great transition for the country and the people. A peaceful era was coming to an end, and a new period of upheaval and violence was just over the horizon. Europe and Asia were tearing each other apart with every indication that the United States could be pulled into a war it was grossly unprepared to wage. The crippling depression had lingered for years with prosperity "just around the corner." The economy did not improve until the nation began to prepare for its own defense against all aggressors.

Over twenty years of peace had passed while the country allowed its military capacity to dwindle to a point where it was almost nonexistent. It was a situation that required a massive infusion of funds and manpower to correct.

The Maine National Guard was receiving more materials and equipment that summer than the total for the past ten years. They were ordered to extend their training and enlistment programs. Soon after Evan appeared in court at the Marshal Lovejoy trial, his infantry company left for intensive training at Fort Drum in upper New York State. They were attached to several other companies forming three battalions so that it could train and maneuver as a full regiment. The training was more intense than in past years. There was an air of desperation within the higher commands. If an enemy attacked the country, current forces were inadequate for a proper defense. The nation was vulnerable, and the Army was scrambling to makeup for lost time.

Evan was a seasoned campaigner who took the potential threat seriously. He trained his company with a sense of urgency, trying to instill that unsettling fact that the country was militarily weak into every soldier's consciousness. They looked up to him for direction. His experience in combat made him a valuable part of the Army team.

At the end of the training program, the infantry company was transported back to Greenville across the northern portion of Vermont and New Hampshire in ten brand new Ford one-and-a-half ton trucks that had been issued to them at Fort Drum. The one hundred thirty men in the company were happy to be back home. A large crowd of families and friends had gathered to greet the returning guardsman.

Evan made sure that all of the equipment and supplies were properly stored and secured before he released the men. They were greeted by whistles and shouts of joyful reunion. The men ran towards their loved ones with open arms. Evan was among them. He spotted Amie and Rena scanning the crowd for him. They had a young man with them that Evan surmised to be Roberta's son, Todd. Rena saw him first and threw herself into his arms. He caught her and twirled her around. She was the joy of his life. He was devoted to her. She was a petite young lady with sandy-colored hair and her mother's gentle disposition and good looks.

"We saw your trucks go through Monson, Daddy," she exclaimed, releasing him. "Aunt Amie drove us to Greenville in your Studebaker Commander. Todd is going to stay with his Uncle Bob and Aunt Joyce for the summer."

Evan turned to Todd. "Welcome to Maine, Todd. My, you look a lot like your Uncle Bob when he was your age."

"I'm glad to meet you, Sir," Todd replied, shaking his hand. He was a wiry-built young man with a confident air and blonde hair. He looked at the rows of ribbons on Evan's chest. "When I finish high school next year. I'm going to join the Army. A lot of my friends are planning to do the same thing."

"The Army can certainly use more good men, Todd. These are uncertain times. I only hope that we have enough time to prepare for the unthinkable. It's nice to see you again. The last time, as I recall, was when you were six or seven years old."

Amie quietly watched his warm reception and held out her arms to him. He embraced his faithful sister. "How nice it is to have you back home, brother. You look handsome in your Army uniform."

"Flattery will get you anything, Sis. I see dark circles under those pretty eyes. I think you may be working too hard at the hospital," Evan told her.

"Hi, Amie," a voice called from the crowd.

Amie turned to see who was asking for her. It was Yertima Ranta, a neighbor and classmate from Monson. She ran to hug him. "It has been a long time, Yertima. How have you been?"

Yertima blushed. He had blond hair and finely chiseled facial features like the rest of his male family members. "We're glad to be home. It was two years ago that I last saw you, Amie. I was hoping that I might bum a ride back to Monson with you."

Amie had always considered him as her best friend in town. They had walked every day to and from school since they entered first grade and graduated from Monson Academy. He was a hard-working farm boy with a wide circle of friends. "We'll be glad to make room, Yertima. Grab your duffel bag," she told him.

He walked with her towards Evan and Rena and said, "You know they've planned an alumni reunion for this coming weekend. May I take you to the dance? It will be like old times."

"I'd have been mad if you had not asked me, Yertima. It will be fun to see some of the old gang again," Amie declared.

Evan liked the mild-mannered Finnish farm boy. "Climb aboard, Yertima. I'm proud of the way you handled your platoon on maneuvers."

Evan drove his Studebaker with Rena and Todd in front with him. Amie and Yertima sat in the back talking about the alumni gathering taking place soon. Evan turned into Yertima's family farm to let him off.

"The first thing I'm going to do is take a steam bath," he cheerfully said, getting out of the car. "Thanks for the lift, Lieutenant."

"You're welcome, Yertima."

When he turned into Bob's driveway, he noticed a Chrysler coupe with New York plates parked in the drive. He assumed it was Roberta's vehicle. He was not sure if he could confront Roberta even after all the years that had passed.

Amie saw Roberta sitting in a chair on the porch and jumped out to see her. Amie and Roberta had remained close over the years, more like sisters than neighbors. "I thought the

New York plates were yours, Roberta," Amie cried, hugging her.

"You haven't changed a bit, Amie. It's nice to be home again, and to see familiar faces," Roberta replied. She looked hesitantly toward the car where Evan was talking with Bob about current world events.

"Come, Roberta. It's time you and Evan buried the hatchet and were civil to each other." Amie grabbed Roberta by the arm and half-dragged her around the porch to the front entrance.

Joyce came out of the kitchen followed by Bob, Jr., their nine- year-old son. Bob was nervous when he saw Amie approaching with a reluctant Roberta. Evan also saw the distressed look on Roberta's face and regretted stopping by at this time.

Roberta met Evan's uneasy glance and cut to the heart of the problem in a wavering voice. "Hello, Evan. Do you think it's possible for two people who once were good friends to ever be friends again?"

Her directness at first threw him off balance, but it was typical of Roberta to face issues squarely. "Harboring hatred has been a tedious task, Roberta. This is not the time or the place to discuss painful events of the past. You may not believe it, but I've always been your friend from a distance. I could never be your enemy."

Roberta was encouraged with his honest reply. "I was going to ask you a favor. The way things look in this crazy world we live in, our Monson alumni gathering takes on a meaningful significance to all of us. The future is quite uncertain. I was going to ask if we could do a duo at the dance. Bob and Joyce have informed me that you continue to play for some events in town. I'm glad you still play the violin. Maybe we can recreate an old tradition. What do you think?"

Relieved that she had made the first move to break the awkward silence between them, he answered, "I'd like that, Roberta. Thank you for asking."

"Thank you..." she cried. Tears formed in her blue eyes as she ran into the house. Young Todd followed after her, concerned for his mother.

Bob was pleased with the exchange he had just witnessed. "Those are the first words you two have had with each other in several years. I want you to know that I understood the pain and the reason that motivated your decision to shut my sister out of your life. That's not to say that I agreed with your choice. The anger that you suppressed was out of character with you, Evan. I was upset with my sister's hasty decisions, but my love for her transcended that judgment. I was hoping that someday I'd see that burden lifted from you because I love you like a brother and supported you in every way possible. It's been difficult to not share what was really in my heart. You built a wall around yourself. The only one to break through that wall was Joleen. I thank God she came into my best friend's life when she did. We all shared and rejoiced in your happiness." Bob placed a hand on Evan's shoulder and continued. "I've been wanting to make that statement to you for a long time. If it offends you, then I'm sorry. I ask your forgiveness."

Amie and Rena understood what Bob was saying. They too had walked a fine line when it came to Roberta. They had enjoyed being with her whenever she visited her brother. The fact that Evan had adamantly refused to acknowledge anything about Roberta made them feel guilty, almost as if they were violating their love for and loyalty to Evan. He had continued to suffer in silence.

In his heart, Evan knew that everything his friend said was true. He embraced Bob. "No man ever had a truer friend than you've been to me. In reality, it is I who should ask you for forgiveness. I've been pig-headed in carrying my hurt pride too far. Thanks for being friend enough to tell me what you really think."

The two strong men clung to each other for several seconds. It was a rare moment of empowerment and renewal of a friendship that had stood the test of time. Joyce was a spectator to what took place and silently thanked God. She took Amie and Rena into her embrace for they, too, were moved by the scene. They had been praying that Evan would be able to shake the yoke of despair that always lingered just below the surface. Tonight the shackles had been loosened and the bond of friendship strengthened.

Evan returned home with Amie and Rena. Joyce had insisted that they take a fresh pot of baked beans and a pan of warm boulla rolls with them. He was a little more restless than usual. Amie and Rena respected his need for reflection and retired to the living room.

Sitting in the kitchen looking out at the moonlight reflecting off the glimmering water of Lake Hebron, Evan finished his coffee and rinsed the cup in the sink. It was a beautiful summer evening with hardly a cloud in the deep blue sky. He poked his head into the living room to announce, "I'm going up to the lookout for a while. Don't wait up for me."

Amie and Rena both understood his desire for solitude that special place always provided. Amie silently thanked God, praying that her brother's time in Purgatory was coming to an end. She had seen a softening of the lines around his eyes after they left Bob's and Joyce's place. His ties to Roberta had never been completely severed. Her presence had stirred old memories that had been dormant for a long time.

The night was warm with a slight breeze laden with the scent of pine and spruce from the northwest. The world was embraced in the solitude of the evening. He breathed deeply of the fresh air filling his lungs and exhaling. How he loved this time of the night when the busy world was hushed and cloaked in tranquility. He sought direction and comfort, hoping to find his place and reason for being in a world that seemed to always be in conflict. Peace of mind was an elusive virtue he was always searching for and rarely found.

As he neared the top of the hill, he had a feeling that he was not alone. Stepping on the large granite outcrop, he looked from side to side. On his right he saw a person half-hidden by the shadow of an overhead branch from the large white pine tree the person was sitting under.

He hesitated and called out, "Is that you, Roberta?"

"Yes," came a soft reply. "I knew it was you before you reached the top, Evan. I'll leave if that's what you want."

"No, please stay, Roberta. I have no right to ask that of you. This has been a milestone day for me. I needed a chance to sort things out up here where one can feel detached from the crazy world that's tearing itself apart."

He took a seat beside her with his back against the majestically gnarled white pine tree, facing the view to the west. Mixed with the resinous scent of the pine tree was a subtle fragrance of heliotrope. It brought back memories from a long-forgotten past, igniting feelings he had denied with bitterness.

Roberta wiped the tears from her eyes, relieved that her presence was not going to provoke a battle of words. She was too tired to deal with the events of yesterday. For several minutes they both drank the beauty of the panorama before them. The moonlight reflecting off the dark waters of the lake below had the power to soothe the soul and to excite the heart.

She was the first to break the silence. "Bob told me that you've been promoted to captain. You've done well, Evan. Bob has kept me abreast of events around town. Things are not looking good for the future. I'm frightened for my son, Todd. He's joining the Army when he finishes high school. By then the draft will be in place."

"He told me the same thing. He's a fine young man, Roberta. The Army is mobilizing at a dizzy pace; my promotion is a part of that expansion. I expect our Greenville Company will be activated very soon. I've worked hard to train it. We just got equipped with brand new semi-automatic Garand rifles at Fort Drum. It's a superb weapon. Most likely our company will be broken up into platoons to act as a nucleus for building other companies and battalions with all the new recruits that are coming out of the training depots."

"Does that mean you'll be leaving soon? What about your position as a game warden?" she casually asked, feeling more relaxed.

He could not believe that he was sitting beside Roberta here at the same spot they had treasured as youthful lovers. For years he had successfully erased her from his mind. Now they were together in that one spot in the world they considered "special." Suddenly he felt as if a heavy emotional load had been lifted from his consciousness. He felt liberated. "My job as a game warden has a much lower priority than my role as a soldier. The country is at grave risk of not being able to defend itself in the event of an attack from either Japan or Germany. The more I learn about our unpreparedness, the more concerned I become. All of the National Guard units will be activated shortly. Our company was rated as one of the best at Fort Drum. That means we'll be one of the first to be called to active duty. When that happens, Rena will stay with my Aunt Mildred until she finishes school. She wants to be an

Army nurse. I worry for her. She's been a blessing to her Dad."

"She's a sweet young lady. I expect she's a lot like her mother, Joleen. Bob and Joyce were very fond of her. I was frightened for you at her funeral, Evan. It was such a tragic ending to something so beautiful. I so envied the life the two of you shared..." she unconsciously bit her lip, regretting the words. "I'm sorry, I did not mean to open old wounds."

Evan was quick to reply. "Joleen and I were blessed with a good marriage, and I'm thankful for our time together. I don't mourn her death anymore. I simply try to live my life so that she would approve. She's gone, and life goes on. Accepting that fact was difficult, but Rena has been able to lift me from the darkness. How I love that girl!"

"You're a strong man, Evan," she said in a wavering voice. "It seemed that every time I came to a crossroad in my life, I took the wrong turn. My first and most monstrous transgression was being unfaithful to the dreams you and I shared for the future. I've regretted that act above all the others. Can you forgive me, Evan?"

He locked every word she spoke into his consciousness. That act had almost driven him insane. It had destroyed his outlook on life and robbed him of the values that had guided him through the war years. For a long time he was like a ship on a rough sea without a rudder. Those poisonous years ended when he fell in love with Joleen. "You'll never know how deeply that hurt, Roberta. How I hated you for destroying what we had together..."

"I knew that," she frantically cried. "I was out of my mind with regret. I'd do anything to erase that sordid act..."

"Forgiveness became possible only after I married Joleen. If it helps, I do forgive you, Roberta. I believe that the woman who was my best friend and that I loved all through my youth, would suffer from her act of betrayal. Who am I to stand in judgment?"

She began to cry. "You'll never know how much those words mean to me..."

He reached out to grasp her hand. "I've followed your singing career from the beginning, Roberta. I have most of your records." He wanted to change the subject to a lighter topic. "With each new song, your voice matured beautifully.

144

Most of the pretty ballads were truly great works of art. I must say that some of the slap-stick ones like *MILLION DOLLAR BABY, JEEPERS CREEPERS,* and *DIPSY-DOODLE* lacked the heart and soul that, for me, has always been an important ingredient in most of your ballads. Maybe my taste is too serious, but music has to cultivate a warm feeling and a lifting of one's soul out of the ordinary. I'm probably not making much sense."

She wiped her eyes again, amazed at the depth of understanding and interpretation he had of music. He was a hard-working man with the heart and soul of a poet. She had always known that his gentle nature was a manifestation of his inner strengths. It had been that intrinsic softness that had won her heart many years ago. What a fool she was to choose Victor and his shallowness over Evan and his inherent goodness.

"You're making more sense than you think. Your intuitive evaluation of my recording career flatters me, Evan. Victor insisted on those songs that were popular. I was reluctant to do them. I'm getting older now and make my own selections. The public likes younger more showy female singers. That suits me fine. I don't do concerts anymore, as you may already know. My recording sessions are fewer and fewer, but at least I'm free to do what I call beautiful music. If my interpretation isn't popular, then so be it. Some songs should be done just because they are beautiful." She shivered. The evening air was cooling.

He was wearing his Army tunic and took it off. "Here let me place this around your shoulders."

"It does feel good, thank you," she answered. "I'm so thankful for this conversation, Evan."

"Where is Victor now?" he asked hesitantly. He knew that he and Roberta had separated several years ago. Todd lived with her in New York. He never knew for sure, but Bob had hinted that Victor did not want any responsibility for his son.

Roberta collected her thoughts and said, "Victor rejected Todd and me years ago. He's living in Hollywood, which is a cesspool of immorality. I refused to follow him and have never regretted the decision. My life has been such a whirlwind. I never knew where I was going. The record sales never meant that much to me. Sure, one has to live and pay the bills. Not much mattered, except Todd. He has been my life. I don't know where I would be if not for him. You'll never know how badly I needed the friendship we shared long ago, Evan..."

He placed an arm around her shoulders and gently kissed her. It was a moment of renewal neither expected. Suddenly, they were captivated by the intensity of their emotions. They were young again filled with promises for tomorrow.

"Oh, Evan," she cried. "Hold me... hold me... I've missed you so much."

"Is this real?" he asked, afraid to believe what his heart was telling him.

Roberta softly kissed his eyes closed. "Yes, it's real. Don't ever let me walk away alone again..."

Chapter Nineteen

Evan and Roberta spent a long time with each other at the lookout. The intensity of their feelings surprised both of them. They were able to laugh and joke about events they remembered from early school days. Evan had teased her about the time she was asked by their fourth grade teacher to name the first President of the United States. She had self-consciously answered, "I don't know, but it wasn't Lincoln," and quickly sat down. The whole class laughed at her.

"I was terribly embarrassed. Mrs. Pennington scolded the class for their outburst. I remember that you did not laugh at my discomfort. I think I fell in love with you then, Evan."

"I remember that you looked so forlorn and shy. Kids can be cruel without really meaning to," he replied.

The revelation of suppressed feelings contributed to a transformation of their outlook for the future. They did not feel alone anymore. They talked a lot about the approaching alumni dance and its importance to the town people at this troubled time in history. They agreed upon the songs they would do together with a finale of *Danny Boy.*

They laughed and cried together. The magic of the lookout was working on the couple. That night it was the stage upon which two lonely people, lost in their day to day journey through life, had found, to their amazement, the pure joy of love reclaimed from the ash heap of despair.

"Where do we go from here, Roberta?" Evan asked. "Is this real or is it a ruse we'll wake from tomorrow or the next day and view things differently? I don't know about you, but I can't take another emotional beating."

She placed a finger to his lips. "Hush, Evan. Let's take one day at a time. Why don't we get together when you can find the time to rehearse the songs? Gee, it's going to be fun to do it with you. I've always been so proud of you and have loved

147

you from a distance for a long time. Please don't shut me out again. I hope you want what we've just discovered as much as I do."

With that they descended the hill, two different people from the dispirited couple that climbed the mountain in search of direction. They had found something more precious than either had bargained for...

The night of the alumni dance took place at the Tarr's Hall on Tenney Hill, a short distance from their homes. Evan volunteered to pick up Joyce, Roberta, and Bob as he dropped off Rena with Todd and Bob Jr., Amie was escorted by Yertima. When Roberta met him on the porch dressed in a dark green dress with her hair falling about her shoulders, his heart filled with happiness. She was beautiful. They laughed and joked with friends and schoolmates and danced several sets together. The occasion was all that they anticipated it to be, and they were happy.

On previous years, it had been awkward if both showed up. Generally, Evan refused to go if he knew that Roberta was going to attend. How he regretted those wasted years filled with anger. Tears filled Roberta's eyes several times during the evening when she was held in his arms. "Now that I've found you, it'll be hard to see you leave home for the Army," she whispered, resting her head against his chest.

He had similar misgivings and held her even closer. "Remember, one day at a time. After this waltz, I want to check my violin in the room beside the stage. I replaced a couple of strings and want to check how they held tune."

She followed him into the room. He had used his old violin for rehearsals. This was the first glimpse she had of the Gottlieb violin given to him by Joleen's father. "What a beautiful instrument," she exclaimed.

"It has a wonderful tone. Mr. Carpenter was a very generous man," he replied, fingering the scale up and down several times.

"The tone is soft and mellow," she agreed. "I think they're about ready for us. It's strange, I've sung in a lot of theatres and halls over the years. Tonight I'm a little struck with stage fright."

He smiled at her. "That makes two of us. Let's do this for the folks who have come to see us. I still remember how it was before I left for France. You'll never know how often I thought about that night when it was rough in the trenches."

She grasped his hand. "Tonight may be an encore of that time many years ago. Come, Evan, let's give them our best."

They began their performance with a favorite folk song, *The Last Rose of Summer* followed by *September Song* and *Harbor Lights*. Roberta's voice filled the small hall and touched the hearts of everyone present. She was a talented performer enjoyed all over the country; yet, she was uniquely Monson's very own. She still had that small-town way of touching the heartstrings with her clear soprano voice. The audience kept asking for more. They did *Over The Rainbow* and *My Blue Heaven*. After the last song, Roberta held out her arms for the audience to stop clapping.

"Thank you, thank you, dear friends and neighbors. How nice it is to be with you tonight, and how very special it is to have our very own Evan Mundy making beautiful sounds on his violin. It's like old times. Now, for our finale, we'd like to do a song that has been a rich tradition at these alumni gatherings."

She reached out to pull Evan closer to her and locked her arm in his. "There are storm clouds on the horizon and we all pray that the vicious battles raging in Europe and Asia will pass us by. Captain Mundy and many others in town may be leaving us soon. Duty calls, and how proud we are of their commitment to defend this country we all love." She kissed him on the cheek and whispered, "This one is for you, Evan."

Evan placed the violin under his chin and played the introduction to *Londonderry Aire*. Tears formed in Roberta's eyes as she became a part of the poignant story of the love of a fair maiden and her soldier about to leave for war. The crowd knew that they were experiencing a performance they would long remember. There was hardly a dry eye in the hall.

Evan was choked with emotion. When he played the last refrain with long steady strokes of the bow, "…Oh Danny Boy, I love You So…" Roberta's lips trembled and her voice broke down. Suddenly, they were transported back to 1917 again. He squeezed her hand and bowed several times to the audience. A long line was forming for friends and schoolmates to come by to shake their hands and wish them well.

Joyce and Bob were the last in line. "I have never heard my sister and my best friend sound as great as they were tonight. I'm so proud of you both," Bob told them.

Time passed quickly. The lazy days of summer were waning in anticipation of fall, giving way to the colorful autumn pageantry that was so much a part of northern New England. It was a time of preparation for the long winters when the land was heavily blanketed with snow. People's social activities were contracted, and family life became the center piece of rural Maine. The death of summer reflected the emotions of the nation on the threshold of being pulled into the cataclysm exploding all around the world. The pulpwood camps of the Great Northern Paper Company were preparing for the winter harvest of wood fiber, and the quarries still employed a large part of Monson's adult male population.

Evan was busier than ever. Two of his wardens had already joined the Army or Navy, leaving him with a heavier work load than usual. He had just returned to his Greenville office when an S.O.S. sounded for assistance on the west slope of Boarstone Mountain. He was one of the first responders. A hiker had fallen off a cliff and was wedged between two large pieces of granite about three hundred feet below the cliff on the sheer walls of the mountain. There was no other way to get to the injured man except from the cliff above him. The ledge at the top of the cliff overhung the wall. The only way to reach the man was by a long rope forcing any attempted rescue to climb back up the rope. Evan was an experienced climber, and it was too much for him.

He suggested to the two wardens, two forest rangers and to Joe Hansen, the faithful deputy sheriff, that if they fastened a pulley between two sturdy planks, it could be placed out over the edge of the granite formation so that the sharp edges of the granite would not severe the rope. That would enable the men on top to lower or lift the rope without any danger to the climber and the injured man once extraction began. It would take a few more minutes to install the pulley, but they saw no other way. Joe Hansen had a new back-pack radio with him and he called for the pulley and two planks.

While they were waiting for the equipment to arrive, they called to the injured man below. There was no response. Evan volunteered to make the descent. He studied the area below

150

and visualized that he might have to remain on the crevice while he fastened the injured man into a harness at the end of the rope. Once the pulley was anchored at the lip of the overhang, Evan was lowered to the injured man. There had been no response from the man to Evan's calls to him. There was not enough room on the crevice for Evan to safely balance himself while he fastened the man into the harness.

The only solution available for him was to secure the man to his own harness, and the two of them be lifted out together.

"Can you hear me?" Evan repeated as loudly as he could to be heard above the screeching wind that swept the sheer west face of the mountain. When he was lowered slightly above the injured man, Evan signaled for them to stop lowering him. The man was wedged in a scissors-like formation. A broken back was a very real possibility. Lifting him straight up by his shoulders was probably the safest way to make the extraction.

"Can you hear me?" Evan cried again, hoping to get a response.

The man blinked his eyes! An encouraging sign! "Yes, I hear you. I can't move my legs," the man replied in a weak voice.

"My name is Evan. What's your name?"

"My name is Frank… I was hiking with some friends."

Evan signaled the rope handlers to lower him a couple of feet. "Well, Frank. I'm going to lift you out of here. You'll soon be in a hospital. Can you use your arms?"

"Yes."

"That's good. Now I'm going to help you fasten this harness around your upper torso. We'll be hoisted up together. The rope is strong enough to hold both of us. Do you understand what I'm saying?"

"It hurts when I lift my arms."

"Be patient, Frank. I'll place the harness over your head. It's important that we lift you out of the crevice with as little disturbance to your back as possible." Evan placed Frank's arms into the harness. Evan was going to use a small loop of rope to tie Frank to his own harness when it slipped out of his fingers and he dropped it. Not wanting to alarm Frank, Evan told him he was going to hold him with his arms face to face for the journey up the cliff's wall. There was no other way.

151

"Now I'm going to signal them to lift slowly. It'll take a steady effort to free you from the confines of the crevice that's holding you. It may hurt, but we have no alternative. We're running out of daylight and the wind is increasing in velocity. I'm going to place my arms around you."

"I'm scared, what if you drop me?"

"You're about my size, Frank. I can do it. Trust me, Frank. If we go down we go down together. If we go up, you're coming with me. There's no other way. I'm giving the signal. We're running out of time."

Evan gave the signal to hoist slowly and grasped Frank in a death-like embrace, locking his hands around his body underneath his small backpack. Frank's body began to rise out of the crevice, but his boots were caught! Frank's dead weight made it impossible for Evan to free them. In desperation, Evan kicked Frank's ankles, loosening the hold the rough granite had on him, and they began their slow ascent up the face of the cliff. It seemed like an eternity to Evan. His arms ached. Once his left arm slipped. He quickly grasped the leather harness strapping and wrapped his legs around Frank as a safety measure. The wind was increasing in velocity as it swirled around the wall of the mountain, twisting them at the long end of the rope.

Their ascent to the top was slow and steady. Evan was proud of the men at the other end of the rope. His trust in them was complete. They continued to pull Evan and Frank up and over the sheave to the safety of the ledge where experienced hands rolled Frank onto a stretcher for the trip down the mountainside. Evan laid on the ground thanking God for the successful rescue.

"You stretcher bearers go ahead. The man's name is Frank. I'll follow shortly," Evan turned on his back and simply closed his eyes, resting his weary body.

Joe kneeled down to offer him a canteen of water. "You did a great job, Evan."

"Thanks, Joe. I'm getting too old for this stuff. I was afraid I wouldn't be able to hold on to Frank."

The two men sat on the ledge watching the sun set, saturating the western horizon with an orange hue. They were moved by the colorful display, remaining silent for several minutes.

Evan spoke first. "I continue to be amazed how such a beautiful place as this can equally be as deadly. This one scared me, Joe. God was with me. That's for sure."

The two men silently followed the trail to their vehicles. Joe turned to speak to Evan. "There's talk that the Greenville Company will be activated soon. I want you to know that I'll miss you when you leave for active duty, Evan. You've been a credit to the Warden Service, and I've been proud to call you a friend. Things don't look good out there. We're coming to the end of an era that will probably never be the same again. That saddens me, maybe because I'm growing older. When you leave, be assured that those of us who are keeping the home fires burning will do our best."

Evan was touched by Joe's statement. He was not one to make rash comments. There was an inherent decency in Joe that generated trust and admiration. "Joe, the people have been well served by you for these many years. I've valued our friendship more than you'll ever know. Thanks for always being there for me. I think I'll stop by the hospital to see how Frank is doing. See you around, Joe."

Late in August, Roberta told Evan that she was returning to New York. Todd had to register for the coming school year, and she was committed to another recording session. She gave him the address and telephone number of her home in the outskirts of Albany near the Hudson River. Evan knew that she would be leaving before the end of the summer vacation. Now that it was imminent, he had that sinking feeling of being alone. He was going to miss her.

The evening before she was to leave, he invited her to dine out. They were anxious to spend some time alone together. He took her to a fine restaurant in one of the hotels on Moosehead Lake near Mount Kineo. Their heads were filled with the question: "What next?" They were facing uncertain times when tomorrow could not be guaranteed. They finished a lobster dinner and relaxed over coffee, enjoying the magnificent view of the water.

Evan told her that his outfit had just received orders to be prepared to ship out to Fort Devens, Massachusetts. "I received verbal orders this morning. We're going to Devens for additional training and replenishment of supplies. I've already given the Warden Service my notice. As of tonight, my duties will be taken over by an older warden from Abbot."

Roberta listened to every word. "I knew that this day was coming," she said, grasping for his hands across the table. "I didn't think it would hurt this much. Our love for each other is comforting for me. I'll hate to see you leave for active duty."

"A part of me feels the same way, Roberta." He reached into his pocket and placed a small box in her hand. "This is for you, Roberta."

She opened it to find an engagement ring and instantly burst into tears. "Will you marry me, Roberta?"

"Oh, yes... yes... I'll be proud to be your wife," she cried in a wavering voice.

"What do you say if we postpone our wedding until things settle down in the world? That will give us something to look forward to," he suggested.

They ordered wine and made a toast to cement their commitment to each other and to their future together.

Chapter Twenty

The war that everyone feared was coming took place without warning on Sunday, December 7, 1941, when the Japanese bombed the Pearl Harbor Naval Base in Hawaii. Evan was at Fort Dix, New Jersey, training with an infantry battalion of which his Greenville Company was a part. He had been training troops ever since he left Monson, shortly after their last alumni gathering a year and a half ago. It seemed longer than that even though he was kept busier than he had ever been in his life. There was a dread that the country might not be ready for the challenge of a war. That dread cultivated a frenzied tempo to make up for lost time. The Japanese had effortlessly gobbled up all the small islands in the Pacific, threatening Australia and New Zealand.

One afternoon right after the world learned that the United States Army forces had surrendered Corregidor and Bataan to the Japanese Army, he received a phone call from Roberta.

"I just had to hear your voice again, Evan. I've missed you."

He had just come out of the field from an exhausting training schedule. "What a pleasant surprise, Roberta."

"I'm calling to see if we can spend some time together. I'm at the Fort Dix Hospitality Center. I just drove down from New York. I have USO clearances for most of the military bases…"

It took a few seconds to register that his Roberta was on the base! "I'll be right over. I'll grab a Jeep at Motor Pool. What a wonderful surprise. I love you, Roberta."

He saw her from a distance, and his heart sang with joy. She was dressed in a dark green dress with a small beret cocked at a rakish angle. Her blonde hair was pulled on the top of her head, making her look taller than she actually was.

She was beautiful, and as usual, she was turning heads of the young soldiers passing by. He swept her in his arms. How fortunate he was to have the love of such a woman.

They embraced for several seconds without a word. It was a moment they would long recall with fond memories. He saw that her Chrysler coupe was parked in the parking lot nearby. He placed a call to his superior, a Colonel Hadley, for permission to leave base for the weekend. The Colonel was a professional soldier, a graduate of Virginia Military Institute. He was comfortable with authority and was well-liked by the enlisted men and his fellow officers. He gave Evan permission to have some time with Roberta, his fiancée, informing him that he would leave orders to that effect at the main gate.

The two left the base in her Chrysler. For an hour or so they toured around central New Jersey, amazed at the extent of fertile flat agricultural land.

"It's some different from northern Maine," Evan commented. "I sure miss the spruce-fir forestland. I've been lonely here, yet most of my time and energy have been expended on training troops. Your letters have been a God-send, Roberta," he told her, squeezing her hand.

They stopped at an inn on a lake shore and treated themselves to a steak dinner. "I don't want to be alone tonight." Evan looked into her luminous eyes.

"Neither do I."

That night their love for each other was consummated in each other's arms. The future was clouded with uncertainty and despair. There was no guarantee of tomorrow. There was only now, today, and that was the reality that was so difficult to deal with. It was a night filled with warm memories that temporarily blocked out the veil of fear that had descended on the nation.

A few weeks after their evening together, Evan was promised leave time around Christmas, but that was cancelled when he was ordered to the Presidio Army Base in San Francisco. The sudden move was accompanied by a promotion to major with a position as the executive officer of a regiment. It was a bittersweet moment. He was pleased with the promotion and disappointed that he did not have a chance to get home for a few days to see Rena. She wrote often to keep him abreast of news and gossip in Monson. Her plans were to finish high school and then enroll in the small nursing school at the Greenville Hospital. Hopefully she would be able to complete the nursing course and join the Army Nurse Corps. Her Aunt Amie had joined the Army Nurse Corps several months prior to the attack on Pearl Harbor. She was now stationed at Fort Sill, Texas.

When Evan's company from Greenville was activated, it became part of a large number of National Guard units all over the country being formed into regiments and battalions. They were better trained than many of the regulars. The readiness of the armed forces was cause for alarm for veterans like Evan.

The regiment he was assigned to at the Presidio was an ad hoc formation of companies from across the country. They were slightly better than raw recruits and were badly in need of additional training. His first order of business was to draw up a training schedule for the regiment. The commanding officer began basic infantry training at an accelerated pace. The troops took the grueling schedule with few complaints, for they expected to be in combat soon against a determined and well-disciplined enemy. The Japanese soldier had a well-earned reputation for tenacity and cruelty.

One evening after a hard day in the field, Evan returned to his bachelor quarters when the phone rang. He rushed to answer.

"Hello."

"Oh, Evan, I'm so relieved to hear your voice," Roberta exclaimed.

"It's great to talk to you," he replied, unfastening his pistol belt and throwing it on a chair.

"You sound tired, Evan. Do we have a bad line?"

"No, I'm just exhausted. It's been a difficult training period. Hearing your voice has made my day. Where are you now?"

"That's why I'm calling, Evan. The USO is setting up shows all over the country for the servicemen. You might not believe it, but I'm in Los Angeles right now. Todd is in the Army at Fort Bragg. I had a chance to visit with him last week."

"I received a nice letter from Todd. He's homesick like most of us. You're certainly traveling a lot," Evan was thinking of how he and Roberta might get together.

"Todd told me he had written to you. He holds you on a pedestal you know. I have good news to share with you. The USO has arranged two shows for the Presidio next week. I'm hoping that we can spend some time together. I've missed you a lot."

"I can hardly wait, Roberta. I did notice a USO poster in the officers' club, but paid little attention to it. You're going to be a big hit for the men. I'm proud of you. Our schedule has been tight, but I'm sure that my CO will grant me some time so that we can see each other. Do you have regular musicians in your troupe, or do you use local talent?"

"The USO uses a lot of local people. For our tours in California they assembled a small orchestra for this troupe. I was shocked to learn that Victor Turin was the band leader..."

"Your Ex?" Evan questioned.

"I had nothing to do with the selection, Evan. I'd back out, but I signed a contract," she was quick to explain.

Evan replied, "I did not mean to pry. It just seemed unusual. Does the head of your troupe know of your relationship?"

"They did, and they dismissed it in their haste to obtain suitable musicians. Are you uncomfortable with the arrangement, Evan?"

The mention of her ex-husband brought back some ugly images. "To be honest, it recalls some bad memories. Other than that, if you're okay with the situation, I can accept it."

"Thanks, Evan. When we arrive in the area for the two performances, I'll leave a message for you. I've missed you," she told him.

Suddenly his euphoria over a chance to see his Roberta was overpowered by doubts. He needed to be reassured. For months he had been running on grit and adrenalin with the full knowledge that the unit he was training was the one he was going to take into combat. That frightening reality overshadowed everything, but always he had the memories of happy times with Roberta for support. He desperately needed that support now.

"Are you all right, Evan?" she cried. "We don't have a lot of time. There's a long line of soldiers waiting to use the phone."

"I'm just exhausted, Roberta. I'll wait for your call. Until next time."

"Until next time, Evan. I love you."

Evan examined the base bulletin board more carefully. They were scheduled for Saturday and Sunday this coming weekend. He immediately contacted Colonel Jeremy Hadley for some time off on that weekend.

The Colonel was glad to grant it. "You, Major, are the first to know. I've just received verbal orders to prepare the regiment for shipment to Australia. Keep it to yourself, but get your personal affairs in order. The schedule of the USO troupe at the Presidio is fortunate for you. Enjoy some free time, Major. I plan to take in one of the shows myself."

"Thank you, Sir. I know you'll like Roberta's selections."

The first show was scheduled for two o'clock in the afternoon in the large auditorium on the base. Evan dressed in his best uniform and showed up at the auditorium an hour prior to showtime. He purchased a bouquet of roses for Roberta and asked for directions to her dressing room. The sergeant in charge of security for the troupe directed him to a door just off the stage. As he approached the room, he met a tall man with black hair hurrying down the hallway. It was Victor Turin. He seemed agitated by something, passing Evan without noticing him.

Evan knocked on the door. Roberta instantly asked, "Who is it?"

"It's me, Evan."

The door was opened by a very angry Roberta dressed in a bathrobe. "Please come in, Evan."

"What's up with Victor? He looked upset about something."

Once inside, she embraced him, holding him close. Her heart was pounding. "We just had a very bad disagreement," she confessed with a sigh.

He held out the bouquet to her, "Pretty flowers for a pretty lady."

She kissed him and accepted the roses. "They're beautiful, Evan, thank you."

My, he thought, she's more beautiful than ever. It felt good to hold her in his arms. The joy of seeing her was fleeting. Something was wrong! Old images flashed before his consciousness. That old feeling exploded in his head again that he had intruded where he was not wanted.

In that moment of disbelief, Victor walked through the door. Evan turned to ask, "Don't you normally knock before entering a lady's room?"

Victor replied, "Only when I need to. Is this the boy from back home, Roberta? Can't he wait to get in line?"

The man's haughty air ignited Evan's adrenalin. He took a step toward Victor with a look in his eyes that frightened Roberta. She stepped in front of him placing two hands on his chest. "No, Evan. He's not worth what you're thinking. Maybe you should step outside. I'll meet you before the show starts."

"If that's what you want, Roberta. At some point in time someone will have to teach Victor boy some manners. I'm always available. Good-bye!"

Evan walked out of the room straight to his bachelor quarters at the far end of the base. He walked aimlessly in a daze, angry, hurt, finding it impossible that the surly Victor had done this to him two different times in his life. Rage allowed him to reach his quarters with a resolve that he had been made a fool of for the last time. Roberta could have asked Victor to leave, instead she asked him. He vowed she would not have that chance again. He ripped his tunic off, collapsed on the bed, and wept for a long time.

He was aroused by the ringing phone. He answered it, thinking it might be Colonel Hadley. It was dark outside.

"Hello."

"Thank God. Evan, this is Roberta. I've looked everywhere for you."

"I don't stick around when I'm not wanted," he exclaimed sarcastically.

"You can't really mean that, Evan."

"Oh but I do, Roberta. Maybe my imagination was working overtime, but my instincts for reading atmospheres has been honed to a fine degree. You asked me to leave, and I granted your request. I don't intend to compete with Victor in any way, shape, or manner. I got the message loud and clear. Goodbye, Roberta."

"Evan, don't do this to us, please... please...."

He hung up on her and buried his head in his arms on the table, consumed with grief.

The next day he showered, dressed in fatigue clothes and headed for the mess hall to eat breakfast. Most of the regiment was on leave for the weekend. He selected coffee and blueberry muffins and took a seat next to the entrance door. He saw Colonel Hadley enter the officer's mess and look around. He walked directly to Evan.

"May I join you, Major?"

"Please do, Colonel."

"I wanted to speak to you about our new orders. The verbal orders are now official. We're shipping out to Australia."

"How soon, Sir?"

"As soon as the Navy has a transport available for the regiment. My informed guess is within five days." He noted Evan's dejected demeanor. "Major, normally, I'm not one to get involved in my men's personal lives, but when I perceive that an officer's personal affairs could have direct bearings on the performance of the regiment, that gets my attention fast. What happened Saturday, Major?"

Evan knew this was coming. He would have done the same thing as the Colonel. Filled with despair and a deep sense of loss, he explained what had taken place at the auditorium prior to the presentation of the USO troupe.

"Did you watch the show?" Colonel Hadley asked.

"No, Sir. I went directly to my quarters." A steward asked them if they wanted a refill of coffee. They both offered their empty cups for more.

"I saw the show. Miss Roberta was marvelous. She has the voice of an angel."

"I would agree, Sir."

"She contacted me about you, Evan. I think you read the situation very wrong. She was desperately begging for a chance to see you alone and explain about what really was taking place. It was primarily about her royalty monies. She granted him half of the amount with a promise that he would leave the troupe and never bother her again. I believed her. She had planned her time around you this weekend. She said she has something very important to tell you. I just left her at

161

the Hospitality Center cafeteria where I was treated to one of her boulla rolls with coffee. She brought them from her home and gave me one for you." Colonel Hadley smiled, placing a fresh boulla roll wrapped in waxed paper next to his coffee.

Evan listened to what his commander was telling him. The aroma from the boulla roll unleashed tears that could not be denied.

"Thank you, Sir." Evan was filled with emotion.

"I'll split it with you," Colonel Hadley smiled. "Let's enjoy it and, then I want you to take my Jeep outside and go to that lady at the Hospitality Center. Don't turn your back on her, Major. She's the real thing."

Evan ran to the Jeep and raced to the Center, where he saw a despondent Roberta sitting on a bench at the front entrance of the Hospitality Center. She saw the speeding Jeep, standing up to see who was driving. She was a vision of loveliness. He leaped from the Jeep into her arms. Suddenly, all of his anguish and those bitter thoughts that held him hostage disappeared in the softness of her embrace.

"Thank God you came, Evan. I died a thousand deaths when you walked out of the room and did not attend the show. Please allow me to explain what you interrupted."

"Colonel Hadley told me what you told him. Forgive me for being so pig-headed. Victor's presence ignited a fuse I've been living with for a long, long time."

She touched his lips with her long fingers, "Hush now. Ugly thoughts of you leaving for the combat zone under a cloud of misapprehension has just about driven me crazy. I was desperate and called the base Chaplain. He was helpful and suggested that I call the Commanding General of the base. I was determined to undo what made you so angry."

He chuckled softly. "You really called the General?"

"Yes. He was most sympathetic. He told me to call Colonel Hadley. The General had already called him about us, and he came to the Center to see me. Colonel Hadley is a fine soldier who thinks a lot of his Executive Officer. I love you, Evan. Don't ever doubt me again."

"I was wrong to doubt you. I almost started a fight with Victor. I could have lost my commission..."

She smiled and kissed him on the cheek amidst howls from soldiers strolling by. "You had him so scared, he was

162

shaking. I had been demanding that he leave the troupe for good. I think you helped him make that choice. Now, let's put that obnoxious creep behind us, okay? He's history, so let's put him where he belongs."

"I had shared my boulla roll with Colonel Hadley. You got him hooked on them," Evan laughed.

"I was hoping that they would remind you of home."

"After I change clothes, why don't we go to the Officer's Club where we can have a quiet lunch and be a little more private?" he suggested. "Have you eaten anything?"

"I haven't been hungry since you burst out of the room. Yes, I'm hungry now. I have something I'm anxious to share with you. I'll tell you after we get to the Club," she explained wistfully.

"Now you've got me wondering." He helped her climb into the Jeep.

Both of them ate heartily from the expansive buffet board at the Club. Evan was pleased to see Roberta clean her plate as if every mouth full tasted good. How he loved this lady! She pushed the empty plate to one side and reached out to trace the lines around his eyes with her soft fingers.

"I worry about you, Evan. This damned war has just started and it has already filled me with despair and uncertainty. Having said that, I have some news that I'm so anxious to share with you."

He grinned at her. "How long are you going to make me wait?"

"Do you remember the last time we were together at Fort Dix? Well, you and I are going to have a baby. I'm pregnant!"

Chapter Twenty-One

Henderson Field Airport, Guadalcanal, September 1942

Evan's Army regiment was added to two other ad hoc regiments to form the Army's Americal Division on New Caledonia Island. Troops were desperately needed to supplement the First Marine Division then on Guadalcanal, a tropical island in the Solomon Island chain with an airfield. It was the first island to be captured from the powerful Japanese, and it proved to be a difficult and costly slugfest. Now the Japanese were planning on retaking the strategically important island.

The Marine Corps regiment under the pugnacious Colonel Chesty Puller was in danger of being overrun when Evan's regiment landed on the island. Colonel Hadley was still on board the transport, sick from malaria. That placed Evan in charge of the regiment for their Guadalcanal mission. They arrived slightly after sundown and were rushed to supplement the very thin defensive line around Henderson Airfield. The soldiers came ashore equipped with two days of rations, ammunition, and water.

Evan reported to Colonel Puller who gave him the impression of having the situation under control. That was contrary to what his division headquarters had related to the Army staff. Thus the desperate effort to place Evan's regiment in the line. Evan had no problem in informing Puller that he had orders to reinforce the perimeter defense line, and he fully intended to do just that.

Puller suggested that they pair two marines with two soldiers all along the line. That seemed to be a logical way of inserting the added strength, and he ordered the battalions to organize the men. Evan also ordered a company of soldiers from the first battalion, primarily Maine National Guardsmen,

164

to act under his personal orders as a mobile reserve to be inserted at any point needed. Puller liked the idea.

"I can confess, I never had the extra men for a mobile fire brigade," Chesty Puller admitted. Some of his superior air was deflated when he learned that the soldiers were supplied with the new Garand semi-automatic rifle.

"How is your supply situation?" Evan asked, telling him how the soldiers were equipped.

"It's pretty skimpy at best," Puller admitted. "We're still using the .03 Springfield which is more accurate. We need marksmen more than we need firepower."

"Well, Colonel, my regiment will give you both as you'll soon find out. I used your .03 in the last war. It's a fine rifle, but the Garand is a superior weapon." He looked out into the dark jungle which was alive with a cacophony of different sounds. "I have a request to make of you, Colonel Puller. I have nothing but respect for the Marine Corps, and for the United States Army; therefore, I want to be up front about the tendencies of marines to refer to soldiers as doggies. I resent it, my men resent it. I'm expecting you to pass the word down the line for the marines to call us soldiers. We are American soldiers and will be addressed as such. Do you read me, Colonel?"

Chesty Puller cleared his throat. "You speak your mind, Major Mundy. I'll pass the word. If you've had the feeling that you're not welcome, let me dispel that notion. I never thought I could hold this line against a determined attack from the Japanese. Your soldiers have given me new hope. You're damned welcome by this marine, Major."

The soldiers had little time to settle into their positions or to get acquainted with their partners on the line when the Japanese made an attack upon their positions accompanied by bugles and loud shouts of "American you die!" They were repulsed several times, yet they continued to assault the position with renewed fanaticism. The battle-weary marines soon envied the soldiers and their new rifles. They had witnessed the intense shield of lead exploding from the semi-automatic Garands, taking a vicious toll of enemy soldiers.

Near dawn, when both sides could see better, the Japanese began an all-out assault against the defensive line with wave upon wave of screaming soldiers racing to breach the American defense line. Evan was proud of his soldiers. This was their baptism of fire and they displayed a tenacity of spirit that Puller's marines admired.

Finally, by mid-day when the last remnants of the Japanese soldiers made their famous banzai attack, they came the closest to breaching the line than any of the previous attempts. The ground was covered with dead bodies and the Garand rifle barrels of the soldiers were cherry red from the intense encounter. Shortly after the last attacker fell, the soldiers and marines sat down to rest, wiping the sweat from their brows with grimy hands. The oppressive heat made them sweat, so that their entire dungarees and fatigues were soaked. They soberly surveyed the field of dead bodies and congratulated each other that they had saved the airfield. Soldiers shared their field rations with their marine buddies.

The battle for Guadalcanal was about to be repeated on every island in the vast Pacific before the Allies reached the Japanese home islands. The Japanese never surrendered. They fought to the last man. It was going to be a brutal and costly road to victory. Shortly after the battle to save Henderson Field, the marines were pulled out of the island, leaving the Army to wipe out the last pockets of resistance.

Sometime after the evacuation of the marines, Evan checked the picket outposts for the night and returned to his quarters in an old Quonset hut where he had two letters from home, one from Roberta and one from Amie who was stationed on one of the large Army hospital ships that would accompany the troops in their advance across the Pacific. She was pleased to learn that Roberta and her brother were married and was looking forward to being an aunt!

He saved the letter from Roberta until later in the evening when he could be alone.

My Dearest Husband,

A few lines tonight to tell you how much I love you and how happy I am to be carrying our child. I pray for your safety. The papers are full of the fighting in the Pacific, and it's impossible to not worry for you.

You'll be pleased to know that I've closed my house in New York State and moved into your home so that I can look after Rena. She's so happy to have a brother or sister. She sends her love. We are getting along just fine. We pray together for her Daddy to be safe. Rena and I have just completed planting the garden. Tomatoes and cukes are my favorites. Bob just gave us a batch of Katadhin potatoes to try out on our newly plowed patch. It's so pleasant to have a chance to work in a garden. I've been away for too long. I'm pleased to be back home with the people we grew up and attended school with.

How proud I am to be your wife. I thank God every day for bringing us back together again. There's a full moon out tonight. I'd like to think it may be shining on you, too. I'll hold you in my heart until I can hold you in my arms again. I love you, Evan.

Roberta

Monson, Maine

May 30, 1942

Evan placed the letter on his small field desk and stretched out on his cot. He was exhausted. Ever since he landed on Guadalcanal, he subsisted on four or five hours of sleep a day. The minute he closed his eyes, the first image to fill his head was Roberta in their house. He recalled that she had always liked working in the gardens even as a small child. One day when they were about eight or nine years old, he spotted her sitting in the middle of the cucumber patch eating cucumbers with a salt shaker in her hand. He had joined her and they both laughed. Cukes never tasted so good as those they shared with each other in the middle of the cucumber patch!

Her love sustained him, and the rich memory bank of times they had shared often brought a smile to his lips. The day she told him she was pregnant, they spoke to his regimental Chaplain about getting married. She had anticipated that possibility by bringing the two wedding bands that belonged to her mother and father. The Chaplain married them that same day with the promise that paper-work could be processed later. He had recorded the ceremony in the regimental log.

The single Japanese plane flew over the base that night as it had been doing every night since Evan had been on the island. The plane dropped a few scattered bombs with little effect, except that the intrusion into their sleep was a nuisance. Each day blended together so that he soon lost all sense of time and place. The stinking, rotting jungle offended his sense of smell. It was so pervasive that a shower or a swim and a sponge bath in the Pacific did not erase the aroma. He never got used to it.

Early one morning, shortly after the marines had left the island, he was quickly awoken by his orderly with word that he was wanted at division headquarters. He dressed, grabbed a canteen cup of coffee, and rushed to the bamboo hut that served as headquarters. He noticed several army and navy officers studying a large map of the Solomon Island area.

Plans were underway to break up the Japanese stranglehold in the Pacific. Each advance toward the home island was dictated by the distance from an airfield that could provide air-cover for the advancing forces. Air superiority or at least parity was an important factor in determining where and when. The staff was considering a move to take New Georgia because it had an excellent airfield at Munda on the southwest corner of the island on a level plateau near the coast with rugged volcanic mountain ranges inland to the north.

The staff needed specific information beyond what they could determine from aerial photos. They were hoping that Evan would lead a small reconnaissance patrol to be inserted on the shore by submarine. The patrol would travel north of the airfield into the higher elevations overlooking the facility. From that vantage point it should be relatively easy to accurately plot the defenses. The staff anticipated that the patrol would need two days on the island carrying supplies and ammunition for that duration. They should avoid any confrontation if possible. This was an intelligence operation, not a raid.

Evan volunteered to take the job and picked five unmarried men from his original Greenville Company. He knew he could depend on them. They drew equipment for the task and were issued brand new Thompson submachine guns. Evan asked the navy for a couple of their high-powered binoculars so that he would be able to determine more accurately the size and caliber of Munda's defenses. Within two hours of his briefing that morning, Evan and his hardy crew were whisked off-shore to a waiting submarine.

The captain of the submarine told Evan that he had orders to put them ashore and to retrieve them forty-eight hours later slightly after darkness. He was given a powerful flashlight to signal the sub that they were ready to be picked up. Their signal was three short blinks of the light.

The soldiers relaxed in the bunks in the torpedo rooms while the submarine negotiated the deadly waters controlled by the Japanese navy. Once they were off-shore of their positions for insertion, the sub settled to the bottom and waited for darkness. The captain suggested that they take advantage of the wait to eat a hearty meal to sustain them for the physically demanding task ahead. Evan and his men gladly agreed, eating their fill. The dessert of the day was strawberry ice cream, a hit with the soldiers. They joked that the Navy had better grub than the infantry.

Evan and his soldiers left the safety of the submarine in a rubber raft and headed for shore. The sailors had fixed their correct direction on a peak in the mountain range, landing the inflatable on a sandy beach. They ran from the craft, silently making their way to the large pineapple grove. There they hugged the ground until their eyes became accustomed to the darkness. The noises from the dark jungle had an unfriendly ring to the men from Maine. The plan was for them to lie low until it was light enough for them to move inland to the higher elevations north of the airfield. There were no roads or trails that could be seen from the aerial photos of the area. Evan suggested that the men rest. He checked the safety on his Thompson and told them that he would take the first two-hour watch.

In the morning they traveled about three miles through thick tropical jungle, crossed three small streams flowing from the highlands, and began their ascent of the sharp volcanic mass that rose above the coastal plain. By noon of the first day, they had climbed unnoticed to a relatively open shelf with an overview of the airfield. Evan told the men to cover themselves with leaves and vegetation of some kind so that their outline was disguised in case observers on the ground surveyed the area.

Their binoculars were strong enough for them to see the features of individual Japanese soldiers. Evan carefully plotted the location of every machine gun, anti-aircraft gun, and the precise location of several heavy coastal cannons pointing toward the sea. He tallied the number and type of aircraft and the approximate number of men stationed at the field as indicated by the number and size of the latrine trenches. Pleased with their ability to collect such accurate information, they moved northeasterly around the mountain for a view of the field below from a different vantage point. Nothing much changed from their original assessment.

They decided to remain in place for the night and strike for the coastal pickup point early the next morning. That night it rained hard, soaking the men. Evan had them huddle close to each other so that they could protect some of their body heat. By mid-morning, the rain stopped as quickly as it had started. When the clouds disappeared, the sky in the east burst with a brilliant orange hue all across the horizon. Sunrise in the tropics made for a spectacular sight they would never forget. They took it as a good omen for the day ahead of them and started their precarious descent of the razor-sharp volcanic mass.

Evan was the lead man picking the easiest route of travel. Every fiber of his body was alert for the presence of enemy troops. He saw the flash of movement off to their right, and kneeled down, motioning for the men to do the same. He saw a Japanese patrol of about eight men making their way through thick undergrowth. He silently signaled for the men to form a line to his right and to his left in case they were discovered.

The enemy patrol veered into their line of travel and literally bumped into the Americans. Evan fired first at the last two men in the single file of Japanese soldiers. They killed most of the Japanese patrol with their first volley. Evan was anxious to leave the scene in case the shots were heard by others at the airfield. As they left the scene of destruction, one Japanese soldier threw a grenade at the retreating Americans. It exploded to the right of Evan lifting him several feet into the air before he collapsed on the ground, oozing blood onto the black volcanic ash.

The man next to Evan turned to fire at the Japanese, killing him before he could throw another grenade. The men circled around Evan's unconscious body, apprehensive that their firefight would draw more Japanese soldiers. They quickly wrapped Evan's right arm tightly to his body with several large bandages each man carried. One strong, husky man passed his Thompson to a buddy and picked up Evan, carrying him as if he was a baby. It was imperative that they leave the scene as quickly as possible. Each man had memorized the route back to their pickup site.

Four hours later, they recognized the sheltered coconut plantation where they had spent the first night ashore. They quickly selected a place where they could see the coast and the beach, and placed Evan's body in the shade of a large palm tree. The soldier who had carried him from the interior was exhausted. When they elevated his head to give him a drink of water, he groaned some. That was a good sign. They did not want to move him any more than was necessary in case of broken bones. They were wondering how they would get his body through the small hatches of the submarine.

They waited three hours for the sun to set. The horizon to the west was ablaze with fiery colors, drenching the undulating water with the red and orange hues that made it come alive. Their anticipation of the relative safety of the submarine for their major detracted some from the enjoyment of the display of color in the western quadrant.

When it was sufficiently dark enough to blink their three spots of light, their hearts were gladdened to see the small signal be returned. They waited, alert to any intrusion of their location, until they saw the shadow figure of an inflatable boat softly run into the sand. Three men carried Evan to the raft while two remained on guard with their Thompsons at the ready. Then they passed the weapons to their comrades, pushing the inflatable off into deeper water. They were free of the menacing enemy stronghold. All helped to paddle to the waiting submarine.

The captain anticipated that there would be a need for medical attention and had organized the officer's wardroom as a sick bay area. Evan was placed on a cage-like stretcher and fastened securely to it. That way he could readily be lifted and inserted feet first through the sub's openings. He was frisked away to the wardroom where two anxious pharmacist mates began the delicate task of cutting off his clothing so that they could evaluate his injuries. The man that had carried him from the mountain looked on with concern.

Evan's right side had taken the full force of the grenade explosion. His body was riddled with jagged metal fragments. Those could be treated by the naval corpsmen, but Evan's arm worried them. It had been severely broken in several places and was attached only by torn muscles. They saw no way that they could save his right arm!

Chapter Twenty-Two

Evan was air-evacuated from Guadalcanal to Pearl Harbor to the Army hospital located at Schofield Barracks where his right arm was amputated slightly above the elbow. The grenade fragments had become infected during his transport via submarine and airplane from Henderson Field to a suitable surgical facility. Most of the time since he was wounded, Evan bounced between semi-consciousness and a comatose state. Throughout that period he was aware that he had lost the use of his right arm. He felt no pain during the operation, but was mentally aware of what was taking place.

The reality struck him when he awoke from the drug-induced world where time and place and presence are often confused. He screamed and was outraged at the decision to remove the arm without his approval. His outburst triggered another administration of a sedative which quieted him. All he could think of was what would Roberta think of him? He was no longer whole… He had not heard from her since just prior to the patrol on New Georgia more than a month ago. It took him several days to squarely face the reality of his condition. The doctors had told him that gangrene had set in, and there was no way that the arm could have been reassembled. As harsh as it was to accept the reality, they were encouraging that, in time, after intense therapy, he would be able to use an artificial arm almost as precisely as before amputation. That message gave him hope, but it had taken a while. Seeing how badly some of his fellow soldiers were wounded, he considered himself lucky and was anxious to prepare himself for therapy.

Evan was right-handed and was unable to compose a letter or write a note to Rena and Roberta that he was doing fine. Finally, he had asked a volunteer at the large hospital to write some letters which he would dictate. It was during this

173

exchange with the young aide who told him that a USO troupe with Bob Hope was scheduled to put on a show at the large parade field of the base. The aide suggested that it would do him good to attend.

Still conscious of his incompleteness, he told her, "My wife, Roberta, did some USO work before she became pregnant. She's now five months along."

"Well, Major, you have much to look forward to. The war is over for you. I know that there are times when you become depressed and angry at your condition, but look around you. That corporal across the room has lost both legs, and your friend beside you is blind. Do not dwell on your unfortunate condition; as bad as it is, you have much to be thankful for."

The day of the USO show, the Army was busy preparing a stage on the parade field by placing two large flat-bed trailers end to end. Midday Bob Hope made a tour of all the hospital wards, spreading cheer in his own incomparable way. He loved the troops, and the men knew it. The hospital volunteer that had written Evan's letters whispered in Bob Hope's ear and pointed to him. Hope immediately walked to his bedside.

"Major Mundy," he announced with his unique smile, "I understand that you've received the Distinguished Service Cross. We're very proud of men like you. I've had the pleasure of doing a few shows with your lovely wife, Roberta. She's an angel with a voice that just grows better with time. I hope you're going to attend our show tonight. It's our way of saying thank you for your sacrifices."

"I wouldn't miss it for the world, Sir," Evan replied. "I'm worried that my wife doesn't know what has happened to me."

"The mails are quite slow in wartime," Bob Hope replied. "I salute you, Major. At least you've marched to the sounds of the guns for the last time. Good luck!"

"Thank you."

Bob Hope left the ward in a flourish. Five minutes later, two attendants entered the ward with a wheelchair for Evan. They wanted to make him comfortable for the show. They wheeled him into one of the private rooms normally reserved for VIP's or severely wounded patients. He was positioned at a window that looked out on the parade field with the stage placed near the hospital. The attendants told him they would be right back.

A few minutes later there was a soft knock on the door. He turned the chair with his left hand. "The door is unlocked," he said.

Bob Hope opened the door with a big smile. "Major, I've got a surprise for you."

Startled by the reappearance of the comedian, Evan was speechless when he saw his Roberta running towards him with open arms. Tears of joy ran freely. Bob Hope carefully closed the door.

"Oh, my darling, Evan. I've been out of my mind with worry," she exclaimed, smothering him with kisses. "They told me about your arm. God has answered my prayers; we have each other. Just tell me that you love me. That's all that matters."

Tears blurred his vision of her, and his lips trembled..."I've always loved you..."

Postscript

The Monson Academy alumni gathering for September 10, 1945, was the most boisterous celebration ever held in the rural small town of Monson, Maine. The guns were silent.

The entertainment for that evening was a repeat of the same numbers performed in 1940. Roberta's voice was better than ever, singing the old favorites with two-year-old Evan, Jr., holding her hand, and Evan, Sr., deftly fingering his violin with his left hand while he made long sweeps across the strings with the bow attached to his artificial right arm. It was a night that eclipsed the performance of five years ago.

The End

Other Historical Romance Novels
BY
Clifton LaBree

A Song for Lisa   A Historical Romance

This is the story of a young American woman captured by the Japanese in the Philippines, 1941. Like most prisoners, she was brutalized and sadistically treated with a cruel disregard for human life. Three years later, Lisa and her companions had reached the low point of starvation and abuse .....

Lake of Three Sorrows   A Historical Romance

A warm spiritually uplifting story of courage, commitment, and sacrifice. This is the story of Dale Cooper, a battle-weary American soldier who served in two world wars.

Flickering Flame   (Colonial Series Book One)

A historical novel, about the Cullen family who settled in Portsmouth, New Hampshire, and their participation in events prior to the French and Indian War. Freedom and opportunity were on the march, but it extracted a heavy price. Frontier settlers were ruthlessly killed and butchered by rampaging Indians lead by French officers and Jesuit priests who frequently incited them to greater levels of inhumanity...

Raising the Torch (Colonial Series Book Two)

A continuation of the saga from Flickering Flame, Colonial Series book one, of the Cullen family in Colonial Portsmouth. This is a moving story of love and sacrifice when a small colony had the audacity to fight for independence from their motherland...

Non-Fiction Books

By

Clifton LaBree

New Hampshire's General John Stark, Live Free or Die: Death Is Not the Greatest of Evils

Publisher - Fading Shadows Imprint

A fresh look at one of America's staunchest defenders of liberty and freedom. John Stark was a courageous New Hampshire citizen-soldier who fought in both, the French and Indian War, and the Revolutionary War. His pursuit of leadership excellence on the battlefield distinguished him as one of the most successful combat commanders of the war, and one of the least appreciated.

His selflessness, modest life style, and devotion to the cause of freedom are an inspiration that time has not diminished. He remains today the embodiment of the frugal, independent, and cantankerous New Hampshire Yankee.

Gentle Warrior, General Oliver Prince Smith, USMC

Published by - Kent State University Press. Kent, Ohio, 2001

The Story of one of the United States Marine Corps best General Officer. His flawless performance in Korea is a story that needed to be told.

FADING SHADOWS IMPRINT

Fading Shadows Imprint was established to bring to the public books of historical events and portraits of people enduring tragic circumstances of by-gone days. Hopefully, they will generate a deep appreciation and respect for the exceptionalness of the United States of America, and an appreciation for the sacrifice and selflessness of those who valiantly served for liberty and freedom.

The characters are fictional, but the historical events and dates have been seriously researched and are factually presented. Some books feature incidents during the French and Indian Wars as well as the War for Independence.

World Wars I and II are eras rich in stories that beg to be told. I've tried to pay tribute to the collective courage and heroism, often unheralded, that has defined Americans in every engagement. It was a time when the immortality of dreams and aspirations were defended by the blood of young men and women. There is a beautiful monument and cemetery in a small French village where thousands of white crosses and Stars-of-David are set in perfect alignment, honoring thousands of American soldiers who gave their last full measure. A large granite slab bearing mute witness to their sacrifice has the following words chiseled in stone: TIME WILL NOT DIM THE GLORY OF THEIR DEEDS. Another monument reads: VIRTUE AND COURAGE ARE THEIR OWN MONUMENT AND REWARD. Those simple words define the American soldier from the dark days of the Revolutionary War to the present. They are an American treasure, unique in the history of the world.

Every generation has its own signature and characteristics that uniquely define them. The World War II generation is defined by the immortality of the ideals and truth they gallantly defended.

The United States has freely given precious blood and treasure to defend the rights of man to be free, and we have never asked for anything in return. No other nation on the planet has sacrificed so much for the noble virtues of liberty and freedom. We hope that the selections offered by Fading Shadows Imprint will touch your hearts and generate a deeper appreciation and love for our country.